10

The Master of Jethart

Over the years, Belinda McLean had heard from her mother, the story of Old Jethart—a house of enchantment in a land of dreams, that each could visit when they were plunged in misery in the back street city brickdust. The plot unfolds in Alice Dwyer-Joyce's inimitable style, creating actuality out of dreams and people out of longings. The mind of a child can race many skies and meet many strangers, from "Old Trad", who teaches trust in humanity, to Mrs. Greastly, who tries to destroy it. In the wonderland of Old Jethart, Belinda's mind awakens gradually to the presence of mystery and danger from the past. The Scottish mist-fingers of the Highlands can reach out from beyond the grave.

In the end, Belinda finds her destiny with the black Master of the house of Old Jethart, and her talisman, the Garry-monkey, plays an important part of her life.

By the same author

Price of Inheritance
The Silent Lady
Doctor Ross of Harton
The Story of Doctor Esmond Ross
Verdict of Doctor Ross
Dial Emergency for Doctor Ross
Don't Cage Me Wild
For I Have Lived Today
Message for Doctor Ross
Cry the Soft Rain
Reach for the Shadows
The Rainbow Glass
The Brass Islands
Prescription for Melissa
The Moonlit Way
The Strolling Players
The Diamond Cage

Alice Dwyer-Joyce

The Master of Jethart

ST. MARTIN'S PRESS

NEW YORK

ROBERT HALE & COMPANY

LONDON

© *Alice Dwyer-Joyce 1976*

First published in the United States of America 1976

St. Martin's Press, Inc.
175 Fifth Avenue
New York, N.Y. 10010

Library of Congress Cataloging in Publication Data
Dwyer-Joyce, Alice.
  The master of Jethart.
  I. Title.
PZ4.D993Mas [PS3554.W9] 813'.5'4 76-2562

First published in Great Britain 1976

ISBN 0 7091 5237 X

Robert Hale & Company
Clerkenwell House
Clerkenwell Green
London EC1R 0HT

Printed in Great Britain by
Clarke, Doble & Brendon Ltd.,
Plymouth

I dedicate this book
to my Mother,
with loving memory

PART ONE

Garry was worried. I tried to tell him that Mother would get better, but he said she looked far more ill than she had ever looked, said her hair was quite grey and it was a bad sign. I argued that peoples' hair was always grey, when they were old, but he would have it that she was not all that old. I must not forget how hard she worked, he pointed out. She never complained, of course, that went without saying, but it made no difference. She was not the complaining sort. Even Mrs. Higgins was always saying that Mother was not strong. She was "a creaking gate," same as Mrs. Higgins herself, who lived in the flat below ours and had terrible asthma.

I sat with Garry on my lap and thought of fat Mrs. Higgins. "Mark my words," was what she said. "Your mum is a creaking gate. She'll still be on her hinges, when the strong ones are dead and gone, you'll see." I could never understand what she meant and neither could Garry. Her shoes creaked all the time, but Garry was of the opinion that she had not paid for them. I knew well that this was not true and I told him so. It was superstition and showed ignorance on his part. He looked up in my face blankly with the corners of his mouth turning down, as they always seemed to be in those days.

We lived in two rooms on the third floor of an old house in the town. You had to climb to the last landing of all and there was a good view from our windows across the miles of smoking grey roofs. The gasometer cut a patch out of the sky in front of us and I could count six church spires and four factory chimneys from the bedroom. The square new block of the hospital was almost on our back doorstep. If I got out of bed at night, to stand by the window, I could see the bright lozenges of the hospital lights and I used to think of all the sick people there, who might be lonely or frightened or dying. Garry was the one, who put the black thoughts in my mind. I tried to remember that a hospital was a place where you went to get better, or to fetch a new baby. Then Garry would say that it was where people had operations and died. He had heard Mrs. Higgins tell somebody one day, that there was a dreadful room there, called a 'mortuary'. You could see the dead people lying side by side on tables, covered over with white sheets and with their toes sticking up, waiting to be put in their coffins. I used to go asleep thinking about it, wake up screaming with fright and there would be Mother, standing by my bed, saying "Don't cry, honey. It's only a bad dream."

At night she braided her hair in two plaits on her shoulders. Her eyes would look very dark and sad.

"Go asleep, my dearie! Look at Garry here, tucked in all warm and comfortable against your side. He'll see that you come to no harm."

Garry stared up at her out of his black eyes and his crew-cut hair stood on end, as it always did.

"Go asleep, honey. It's only the wee sma' hours. The cocks won't crow in Old Jethart for three hours yet."

"Tell me about Old Jethart, Mother."

"My goodness gracious, my wee daftie! You know all about Old Jethart by now. There's nothing left to tell you."

"Please, Mother! Tell me about the white gate again and the avenue winding in to the house . . . and the horses coming and the ponies too, to gallop along beside you, as you rode along the grass verge."

It was pronounced more like "Jeddard" with a hint of a 't' in it and it was a good Scots name. It was Mother's way of escaping from life in a two pair back apartment in a near slum tenement. It was a dream of a happy land, another way of life, a wonderful country, where I might live happily ever afterwards, if only I could find the Alice-in-Wonderland way into it.

"Very well, honey, I'll tell you how it was."

She would settle Garry more warmly against my side and take my hand in hers.

"The front gates were white in the grey stone wall and they had a grand kind of a lock. You only had to lean down from the saddle and press back a lever. It unsnipped the catch and there was the gate ready to be pushed open. Of course, you had to remember to shut it again. That was for sure. The fields were full of stock. It wouldn't do to have them stravaging out on the mountain road."

Garry always looked up at her in his blank black-eyed way and we both listened to every word she said. Her Irish voice was soft and pleasant, very soothing too. Mother would be away in Old Jethart and I, finding it hard to keep awake.

"Lady Gay wouldn't have her mind on whether the gate was left open or not. There was a patch of long grass, that she'd get her eye on. She'd want a mouthful at all costs and I'd be a bad horse-woman if I gave way to her. You had to keep a tight hold on her head."

I, who had never sat on a horse's back in my life, never failed to ask if Mother rode Lady Gay in a snaffle or in a double bridle and I knew that the double bridle had a steel curb chain under the mare's lip.

"Lady Gay always went in a snaffle, honey. Wasn't her mouth as soft as silk? You should remember that."

There was a bridle track along one side of the drive, You cantered your horse on it, going out, but when you came home, you took it slow. You must never bring a mount in sweating. There was a yard-man called Rob and if the horse was too hot, it was his job to walk it up and down till it cooled off and there'd be hell to pay. So Mother always walked Lady Gay home very quietly and looked down to her right, to the wide Scots river, that ran round the base of the hill. It was full of salmon and trout . . . a delight to a fisherman's heart. There were deep pools and waterfalls too, places where the water was smooth and silent and deep, places where it was shallow and rushy and singing. There was one spot, with grey stepping stones. You could come dry-shod to the other side. Here the best cowslips grew, year after year. There were primroses in clumps along the bank and a hollow, that turned blue every year, when the bonnie bluebells bloomed. You could stand by the river and see the grey house above your head, the white front door, the six shallow steps, the mountains all silent behind it. The brass knocker winked down the steep at you, if the sun was out and maybe Cousin David would be waiting . . .

The world of Old Jethart was quite another place from the town where we lived. Here, the only green places were the public parks, where you must not walk on the grass, nor yet pick the flowers. Mother was contemptuous of such places, having been born and bred in the country. In Argyll and in Ireland too you might walk where you pleased on the green hills, that ran to the mighty mountains. If you'd a mind, you could pick all the flowers, you saw. It was better to leave them growing in their beauty, cowslips, bluebells, primroses, but there was purple heather too, and rowan branches with berries as red as blood, hazel catkins, fronds of light green bracken.

Mother had been staying at Old Jethart on holiday, when she met my father. There had been a Hogmanay Ball and Father had "swept her off her feet". I know every single detail of that ball, or think I do, and I never hope to see anything so glorious, if I live to be as old as Methuselah. The ladies were from the houses round about, all slender and graceful in long dresses, soft pastel colours. Every one of them wore her clan tartan in a stole draped over her shoulder. The gentlemen defy description in the splendour of their kilts, with lace at wrist and throat, with dirk in stocking top. They danced reels and strathspeys and the pipes skirled till the dawn.

Father had asked Mother to marry him before he had known her for three hours. It was a tornado of a courtship and marriage and it ended in disaster for Father was dead within five years.

"And you never went back to visit Cousin David at Old Jethart?" I asked, knowing that the answer was no.

Cousin David still lived in the house on the hill with a housekeeper to see after him now that "poor Con" was dead. Con was my aunt, Mother's sister. She had been house-keeper at Old Jethart and that was how Mother came to visit there in the first place, for the spring and summer of one perfect year. They had been very beautiful, or so I gathered, Aunt Constance and Mother, though she never said so.

"Tell me about Cousin David. What's he like?"

"I've told you a thousand times, honey . . . tall and black-haired. People thought he was very handsome."

"But not as handsome as Father?"

She always looked shocked at that.

"Nobody was as handsome as your father, Belinda."

"But what was Cousin David really like?"

"Shy and reserved. He never had a word to say for himself. He was kind and gentle. I never did meet a man so kind."

Maybe, if I asked her, she would tell me that he was even kinder than Father had been. Father was a soldier and soldiers aren't kind, or so Garry thought. They are gallant and so brave that there's nothing could frighten them, but not particularly kind.

Cousin David was the same age as Mother and I took this to be very old. I asked her many times, if she would not write to him and tell him where we were. I had visions of going to

Old Jethart to live with him, had visions of seeing Mother ride Lady Gay again, and not do all the hard work she did now.

That always drew her dark brown brows down into a frown.

"One doesn't ask for charity, honey. What kindness or good did I do for him, that he should support me and my child?"

Sometimes, when I talked to Garry, I said it might have been better if Mother had married Cousin David. Then we might be at Old Jethart now, with ponies to ride and the river to fish. If Mother had married Cousin David, Garry said with scorn, I would never have been born, never in any circumstances, past, present or future. I would just never have been. He was put out with me, reminded me that we had no close relatives. If Mother were to die, he and I must be put in an orphanage. There were children at school, who came in every day from Oakland's Childrens' Home, which was out on the Harlton Road. They were happy enough after the first few weeks, when they were red-eyed and quiet. I argued that they were well-dressed and well-cared for, but Garry said they weren't happy. One day, we might find ourselves in Oaklands, if Mother got so ill that she could not support us by the dressmaking she did . . . or worse, if she were to die . . . He made me miserable very often by such talk, but it was beyond my power to stop him.

My early years were passed with the rattle-chatter-whirr of the sewing-machine in my ears. Even now, the sound of an old treadle machine will bring the room into focus again. I can see her again, her dark head down-bent, as she stitched on some bridal dress, altered some child's clothes, turning our worn sheets, sides to middles. Sometimes, when I had been in bed a long time, the rattle-chatter-whirr came through the walls. Then Garry told me that Mother was killing herself with the way she worked far into the night. Sometimes, I lost patience with him and threw him down to the foot of the bed, told him that he was only a stupid toy monkey, who could not possibly know anything or have any thoughts whatever. Then after a bit, I would get sorry for him out there in the cold. Another minute and I crept to fetch him back into bed with me, my mouth against the stubble of his crew-cut hair. Many a night, I wept my fear into his sawdust chest.

Every day, I went to the Council School and I was happy, even though I knew I might be happier far in Old Jethart than in the cheerless asphalt play-yard. I found no difficulty with my lessons and Mother hoped that I might win a scholarship to the High School . . . perhaps even to the University in time. Her dream was that I "would retrieve the fortunes of the house". My ancestors had been scholars and poets, she told me. It must be in my bones to be wise and quick at my lessons.

She was very light-hearted and gay sometimes, especially if we had been talking about Old Jethart. She had gone there when she was eighteen and she cannot have been very old now, but her hair had a white wing in the front. Her eyes were blue and her nose had a tip-tilt to it that made her look happy even when she was sad. She had slender fingers and pretty hands. Her grandmother's signet ring was always on her right little finger, which may have been ridiculous for a dress-maker in a poor district.

Looking back now, I think I was quite unspoilt. My clothes were made over from bits and scraps. The dresses were turned and altered, while they would hold together. We made great use of ribbons and Mother reminded me about the Christmas Carol and the Cratchitt wife and daughters. She and I were "brave in ribbons" too. Our food was of the Cratchitt variety too, but I never recall anything so grand as a goose for Christmas. We had a box of crackers on the tea table and a stocking on the mantelpiece. It must have put her to the pin of her collar to find something to fill it.

She was a good Irish housewife, for she was born and bred

in Ireland, although her people were Scots. We had scones to eat and home-baked bread, jam and jelly on rare occasions. It is a hazy memory now and patchy and dim, but I have an idea that bread and dripping was our main standby, eked out with soups and stews. Sometimes, one of the customers, who owned a shop, gave us the remains of a joint or maybe a ham bone and that was a red-letter day. I think we were very poor indeed, but I may be looking back through the magnifying glass of a child's memory.

There were plenty of the other children at school, just as poor as we were. The odd shop-keeper's child might have a bicycle or a leather satchel, a pencil box, good shoes. If the rest of us envied this, we did so secretly. I might have fared worse in a richer area. As it was, there were plenty of others to sit in the play-ground eating sandwiches, while the chosen few grumbled about the banquet of school dinners. Mother would have tucked two slices of home-baked bread into my satchel, with a wealth of dripping safe between them. There would be a medicine bottle, well-scalded out and filled with milk, sometimes a hard boiled egg and salt with it, in a twist of paper.

"Milk!" she would say with a smile. "You don't know what milk is. In Ireland, aye, and in Scotland too, the milk stands in earthenware vats for the cream to rise, against the churning. There's a tin cup with a curved handle, that you can dip into it. You've never tasted anything like it in all your born days, with the richness that's in it."

I suppose that she did me a disservice in harping on Old Jethart. I was puzzled that she never talked, or only rarely about her old home in Ireland. She had spent the happiest time of her life in Scotland for those six months, and she had been caught up and imprisoned in the bubble of her memories. Garry sometimes said that she had probably been unhappy in Ireland, that there was a mystery about it, but that was just Garry-monkey-talk and I tried not to heed him. The net result of it all was that I was caught up too in the Shangri-La dream of Old Jethart. I must escape from my present position at all costs. High School first and then University, these were my goals. I must find a land flowing with milk and honey, or that is what we planned, Mother and I . . . and this land resembled Old Jethart in every particular.

I was a healthy child. The school doctor could never find anything the matter with me. I felt humiliated when she searched my head for nits, but I did not blame her for it. There were plenty of dirty heads in school. Mother washed out my hair in carbolic twice a week and she had strict rules on hygiene. I had to wash all over every day and my clothes were spotless. I was healthy enough, but she was never strong. It was the one subject that Garry could get me really worried about. She went to the doctor's every month to fetch her heart pills. Mrs. Higgins told her husband one day that Mother had a bad valve in her heart. She explained it to him as a leaky place, like you might have in a pump. Garry and I were listening to every word she said and it frightened us both to death. The blood rushed back instead of going straight on. Mrs. Higgins had seen all about it on Telly. That was why there was that plummy colour to the cheeks and lips. There was an operation for it, but it was no good putting a patch on perished rubber. There was a danger of flying clogs too. This terrified Garry out of his sawdust wits, although he couldn't understand why a clog could get anywhere near the head, where Mrs. Higgins said it lodged. Mother never wore clogs in her life.

I asked Mother about it, all the same, told her it was to put Garry's mind at rest and she laughed and asked me when I was going to stop using Garry as a whipping boy.

"You're an old-fashioned child, Belinda. Don't fret about me and my heart. Cousin David always said it was in the wrong place."

"So he knew you had a bad heart?"

"He knew nothing of the sort. I was as healthy as a snipe in those days. The year your father died, I had the rheumatic fever. Our troubles all came together. It's the fever that made it bad, but it's nothing to worry about. It's fine now."

Garry prompted me to go on with it.

"But you get breathless on the stairs these days."

She looked at me keenly.

"Do I? I hadn't minded it myself."

Garry would not let me leave it alone.

"Your feet swell at night. Your ankles are all over your shoes."

She turned her back on me and told me it was just from the standing.

"They're grand in the morning, when I haven't been on them."

I caught the dark look from Garry's boot-button eyes.

"What would become of Garry-monkey and me, if you were really sick?"

"I daresay Cousin David would come riding down here after the two of you, put you up on the front of his horse and spirit you off to Scotland . . . to bonnie Argyll, where you'd live happily ever after . . . you and your worrying monkey."

She picked him up and admired him, straightened his yellow sweater and set his cap a-tilt on his head.

"It's a pity the hair never grew after you cut it that day. Wouldn't you have thought it would, with all the black thoughts that come out of his head?"

All the same, she began to go to the doctor's every week about this time. Garry brought out all the black thoughts his monkeyish brain could devise and there was no refusing to listen to them, no matter how hard I tried. She had written a letter to somebody too and it had taken her three days to get it right. She tore up twenty pages, before she got the letter she wanted and then she posted it herself, a thing she never did. I offered to drop it in the box for her, but she told me she had to see the man in the corner shop about something. The moment she said it, I knew it was a lie. She put on her coat and tied a scarf about her head, went off downstairs with the letter in her hand. I sat looking at Garry-monkey's face and knew the ideas that were forming in his mind. There was a cardboard box, that Mother had covered with cretonne to act as a waste paper basket. It was a wicked thing to do to pick out the torn scraps of note-paper she had used that day, and jig-saw them together on the table, but I did it. The writing was not easy to read. I was used to print and copper-plate. I made out "after all these years," and "she is very good", and "like her". Then my heart stopped short and re-started with a thump, for I made out the words "Dear Cousin David,"

She had written to him and had not told me. I felt like a thief for having looked at the torn-up letters, but I knew that she ought to have confided in me. I put the last scrap of paper to the jig-saw and waited for her to come back and there was foreboding in my breast, that I could in no way, palm off on Garry. She came in at last and she was very breathless. Her lips were as purple as grapes, cheeks deep mauve, her breath quick gasps, hand up to clutch her coat. She was trying to smile and making a bad job of it.

"Give me my new tablets, honey . . . the wee white ones . . . quick as you can . . . please."

She chewed one of them in her mouth very fast and sat down limply on the kitchen chair, picked Garry up from where he lay on top of the table, glanced at the torn paper and did not see it. I put on the kettle to make a cup of tea and came back to watch her, as she smoothed the wrinkle's in Garry's yellow jumper. She was not thinking of what she was doing, just concentrating on the pain in her chest and waiting for it to go away. Then she looked at me and my face must have told its own story, for she smiled and told me that she would have to knit up a new jumper, as soon as maybe.

"He's spilt some milk down his front, the wild boyo," she said with a wraith of a laugh. "Run to the other room and fetch the bag of wools. We'll choose what colour to give him this time."

I stood by the table till the pain had gone. I knew when she was better with the way the peace came back to her face. It was a bad time to put the question to her, but I put it anyhow, in the terror that consumed me.

"Why did you write to Cousin David?"

She gave me a startled glance and asked me what made me think she had done such a thing and she went on smoothing out Garry's yellow jumper. I picked up the torn scraps of writing paper and put them down in front of her. She took the scrap that had his name on it, studied it for a long time in silence. Presently she asked me how old I was.

"You know how old I am," I said gruffly. "I'm nine years and three months. I'll be ten on the seventh September."

"It's a great age," she sighed. "It's time that you knew it's a wrong thing to read other peoples' letters, even torn-up ones."

I hung my head and mumbled that I knew it was wrong, but I was big enough to share any worries. I asked her to tell my why she had written to him, because something must surely be wrong to make her do it. She got up slowly and walked over to the fireplace, straightened the butter-box stool, that was my special seat and covered grandly in red velvet. Then she took off her coat and undid her scarf, put them away, turned round and smiled so sadly that I had a job not to run across the room and throw myself into her arms. I knew it might be a babyish action and not that of a grown-up person, capable of sharing worries, so I stayed where I was.

"I daresay it's Garry-monkey, who's doing the worrying?" she said.

"It's a lie about him being worried," I said. "It's time I stopped blaming him, for I know well he's made of sawdust. I must sound childish with the way I go on about it, when we both know well that it's me, but I'd be glad if you'd tell me. Please tell me, Mother."

She went to make the tea, for the kettle was boiling, but I told her to sit down again and I took the kettle from the gas stove and poured a little of the water into the brown tea pot and then I emptied it into the sink and put in two spoons of tea and added the boiling water. I spread the white cloth on the table and put the tea pot on it and went and got the cosy and covered the pot with it. I put the scones on the table and the blue bowl of dripping and I asked her if she would care for an egg, because there were two left. She shook her head and I thought that she was not far from tears. I wanted to cry, myself, but I tried to concentrate on setting out all the supper things correctly. I got out a jar of potted meat paste and then I cut bread for toast and put it under the griller. I put out the two blue cups and saucers and the bowl of suger and the jug of milk. I made the toast just as she liked it and spread it with dripping and I cut it into fingers and put it on a plate, and at last I brought it over to her. A tear splashed down on the toast she had picked up, but I thought it best to pretend not to notice it and I went away across the room to get the other chair for myself and set it in place and then I poured out the tea, putting in just a little milk in hers, for that's how she liked it.

"It's nothing to worry about," she said in a queer voice and then she took a bite of toast and tried to chew it, but it lasted a long time in her mouth. I had put dripping on my scone and eaten up every crumb of it, before she spoke again.

"You asked me what would become of you, if anything were to happen to me," she told me. "It set me thinking."

I asked her if she had written to tell Cousin David about us, for she said nothing for a long time.

"I told him a part of the story, said I was sorry not to have written sooner, but it was best. I told him about your father and that I wasn't well. I asked him if anything was to happen to me..."

She paused to drink some tea and I felt the cold fear, heavy in the pit of my stomach.

"I asked him if I could leave him something in my will," she said with the queerest little laugh I had ever heard.

I asked her how she could make a will. Poor people don't make wills, for they have no possessions.

"I have one treasured possession, more valuable than all the gold in the world. There'd not be enough money to buy it, if you saved up all your life."

"That can't be true," I cried. "What have you got that's so special? Why are we so poor? Why would you want Cousin David to have it?"

"He's my first cousin and my only kin. It might seem like making a recompense to him."

I stared at her in amazement. She would see me poor and leave this wonderful gift to him, this rich beautiful possession, which she had never told me about.

"Is it a magic thing, like Aladdin's lamp?"

"It's you honey, I've asked him to look after you, when the time comes."

I jumped to my feet and stood there staring at her. Then I remembered the soft words about the value she set on me, about the love she bore me. I went round the table and buried my head in her lap and we clung together, for a long time. Then we said how foolish we were and dried our eyes. I wet my clean handkerchief at the tap and brought it to cool her face. The tea got quite cold, while we mastered our emotions. At last, I went back to my chair and crumbled a scone.

"He'll come here to see you, when he gets that letter," I said. "Perhaps he'll take us both to Old Jethart and we'll be happy. You can show me all the things, the white gate and the river and the horses and the grey stone house. Do you think he'll come right away?"

"I didn't tell him where we were," she told me shortly. "He's to put a reply in the Personal column of *The Times*, if he wants to say 'aye'."

It took me some time to understand this, for I did not know what she meant. I found out that he would have to pay to put a letter back to Mother in a special part of *The Times* paper, and we must go to look at it in the Public Library every day from next Monday.

"I don't want you to begin to worry about me," Mother told me. "And I don't want to worry Garry either, for the dear knows, that creature must be worried out of his wits, with the way he goes on. The doctor has been fussing about me for years and I still go about my business and I feel perfectly well. It's just that I'll be happier in my mind to have it all settled. I didn't want you to know about it, but it was only because I forgot that you were so grown-up and it's a comfort to have you to share any problems that crop up, and that's a fact."

I saw the answer in the library copy of *The Times* on Monday, bought a copy in a shop to bring home to her. I had to go right down to the centre of the town, but I got it at last. She was very happy when she saw it, because it meant that Cousin David must have telephoned the paper in London to get it put in at once and that showed that he had not forgotten her. She was gay the whole day after that, and I thought that she looked very pretty, as she sat there reading it, her eyes very bright.

"MARY STUART." it said. "IT IS VITAL THAT I SEE YOU AT ONCE. I AM TOUCHED AND VERY GRATEFUL FOR THE BEQUEST. PLEASE TELL ME WHERE YOU ARE, SO THAT I CAN CONTACT YOU AT ONCE. LOVE. COUSIN DAVID."

She got out the writing paper and she hummed a little tune. She wrote a sheet and tore it up, wrote another.

"He'll watch for the post-man in two day's time. He comes up the brae on a bicycle as old as himself, the post-man. He has long white whiskers like Santa Claus."

"Are you going to tell him where we are?"

"Not yet, honey."

She went to the mantelpiece and took down an envelope from behind the clock. She held it in her hand and looked at it as if she wanted to make up her mind about something.

"There's a telegram inside here," she told me at last. "It's filled in and addressed and all ready to go. The money's with it. If anything were to go wrong, you're to go to the post office on the corner. Give it over the counter . . . the telegram counter. Then come back here and wait. Not the next day, but the day after that, Cousin David will come for you."

"Oh, mother, don't talk about such things. You'll be very ill, or even . . . What could I do without you? Don't ever leave me. Please don't ever leave me. I'd be alone in the world."

"You're not to fret. I explained to you that there was nothing likely to happen to me, and you needn't think it will. It's just to put our minds at rest, and Garry's mind too, of course, for we can't have him fretting. It's just a sensible precaution and I've written a letter to Cousin David to tell him what I plan to do. I'll post it tomorrow and his mind will be at rest too. He's a man of his word and he'll come for you, if need be . . . and now it's high time for you to go to bed . . ."

She came to tuck me up later and when I was on the verge of sleep, she sang to me as she often did, in a light soft voice. Her face was happy and peaceful and her mind at rest.

"I had a little nut tree, nothing would it bear
But a silver nutmeg and a golden pear,

The king of Spain's daughter came to visit me,
And all for the sake of my little nut tree..."

When she thought me asleep, she went back to the other room and I clutched Garry-monkey tightly against my chest and moved my lips against the stubble of his crew cut. How could I get out of the habit of confiding in him or he in me? We had done it for so many years. It was my duty to contact Cousin David, I told him. Mother was ill. She would never have written to Cousin David unless she was very ill indeed... and like to die. My mind shuddered from the thought. I had only to open the envelope and look at the telegram. I could put it back again. It was wicked, but it was the right thing to do. When I had the address, I would write to Cousin David and tell him where we were. Yet I was afraid to do it. Garry thought I was a coward and indeed I was. He demanded a definite date, when I would promise to open the envelope and we quarrelled about it. At last, I said I would do it before the end of the week and that seemed to satisfy us both.

I did not worry much the first few days. I went to school in the morning and came home every night. One evening, I picked the envelope from behind the clock and felt the money inside it. There was a packet of envelopes just the same in the table drawer. I had only to put the telegram in one of them and Mother would never know what I had done. I decided to ask Cousin David not to tell her.

Then one night, I opened it, my face red with shame at what I was doing. I read the message and was filled with a sudden foreboding of awful things to come. The message made my heart stand still...

SUTHERLAND, OLD JETHART, INNISH, ARGYLL, SCOTLAND.
MARY STUART DIED TODAY. COLLECT BEQUEST WITH UNDYING LOVE.

I thought I was going to get sick. The sweat stood on my forehead, as I put the telegram into a fresh envelope and pushed it back behind the clock and the clock itself felt angry at me and ticked loudly in the still of the room . . . wicked girl, wicked girl, wicked girl . . .

I had only to remember one word of the address and that was Innish. I knew the rest of it. All I had to do now was to write the letter and buy a stamp, post it at the corner box. What had she meant by her undying love? Surely she had not loved Cousin David? It might explain the mystery of why she spoke about Old Jethart at the time and never about Father. That was all nonsense. Of course, she loved Father. Had it not been a whirlwind romance? "Undying love" after she was dead . . . for that was what it would mean, when the message reached him, could only be something like "Dear somebody" in a letter, which was just the ordinary way of starting off to write, like "yours faithfully" or "yours affectionately" at the end. It was just what the English teacher called a "figure of speech."

My letter was still to write. I waited till a day when Mother had to go across town to fit a lady with a bridal dress. I knew she would be a long time and I had spent days getting what I wanted to say to Cousin David clear in my head. When I came to putting it down on paper, it evaded me and it came out a smudged, ill-spelt cry for help. I was becoming a creature of deceit and lived with shame. The envelope had to be hidden in my school books and posted on the way to school in the box on the corner. I was just popping it in, when Mrs. Higgins came down the street and gave me such a turn that I might have fallen dead at her feet with the shock of seeing her.

"What you doin', Belinda? Posting a letter for your mum then?"

I nodded my head and was liar as well as deceiver and cheat.

That evening, Mother was specially nice to me and I felt more guilty than ever, but there was no going back on my action now. The letter was in the post. As for Mother, she had made a surprise present for me, and she held Garry up that afternoon as I came through the door.

"There's a new pair of trews for His Majesty and a cap to match it. Maybe I should have made his jumper first, for I'll have to wash the milk stain out of the garment he has on. Still, I'll get round to it after the week end. I've got a skein of yellow that's like the sun shining on ripe wheat. He'll be the smartest Garry-monkey in the whole town, so grand that maybe he'll not talk to the likes of you and me."

I was never to know if he would have been so grand, for he got no new jumper after all. On Monday I walked back from school, swinging my canvas satchel by the strap and I was wondering if Cousin David had got my letter yet. It should have gone up to Edinburgh by the Royal Scot. Mother has described the journey so often that I knew it by heart. It should have reached Old Jethart this morning, if it was on time. The old post-man would surely have delivered it, although Mother had told me that he often saved up the post till a few letters collected, before he came out from the town. I imagined the grey stone house and the way Cousin David might at this very moment be looking up the times of the trains south. I turned into Pride's Row and there was a car parked outside our house. For a moment, I thought it was Cousin David arrived and I ran. He might have got the letter on Saturday evening, motored down, all Sunday and all today. I ran as fast as I could, but I stopped short at the door, for it was the doctor's car. Mrs. Higgins had obviously had another of her attacks. She was always sending for him and he used to be angry with her, because she slept in a feather bed and that was bad for a person with asthma. Mrs. Higgins had told me all about it.

"Don't send for me again, while you're in that bed," he had

warned her on his last visit. "For I shan't come, and if I do, I'll pack you off to the hospital."

There was a policeman at the hall door. I went up the three hollow-worn steps and he looked down at me from his great height. There was a small cluster of women in the hall behind him.

"Here she comes now," said one of them and they drew closer together, as if somebody had pulled a purse string.

The policeman asked me if I was Belinda McLean and Mrs. Higgins came huff-puffing down the stairs and said "Of course she is, the poor little ducks," her voice hoarse and wheezing and her eyes pink. She held out both her arms to me, but I dodged past her and went up the stairs like a rabbit. I saw it all in a flash. There was something wrong with Mother.

"You can't go up there, Belinda," shouted the constable and he came running up after me, but I was round the turn of the landing, terrified in a nightmare way.

"Come back here," he called. "Come back here this minute. I want a word with you."

I met the doctor on the second flight and he put out a hand to grab my shoulder, but I twisted out of his grip and pushed past him, so that he staggered back against the wall and got tangled with the constable.

When I came to the top landing, the door stood open and I ran straight into our living room without stopping. There was a second policeman writing, his helmet tall on the table beside him. There was something on the couch, covered with a blanket from the bedroom and I knew it must be Mother. I pulled it back and saw her lying there, with her eyes open and dim. Her face was the same dark mauve colour and her lips were purple grapes again. I grabbed at her hand, but it fell sideways and dangled limply on to the floor. I almost screamed out in my terror. I just managed not to do it, and that was when the strange sensation began. I was not inside my body, but standing looking down on a little girl, who looked like me, but felt nothing. I was walking about on the ceiling, looking down at everybody, looking to see what they would do and what they would say. The little girl put the blanket back gently on Mother's face and looked up at the policeman.

"Garry's been worrying that this might happen. He's been talking about it and wondering what would become of us if Mother . . . She is dead, sir. Isn't she?"

Garry had been sitting on the mantlepiece and I picked him up and hugged him very tightly against my chest with both my arms and I thought how badly he must be feeling. I tried to tell him that we still had each other and got remarkable small comfort out of it. The other policeman came running into the room and picked me up in his arms.

"There now, sweetheart. Don't take on about it. Your Mum is safe in heaven at this very moment and she's as happy as can be. She'd not want to see you crying."

"I'm not crying, sir," I said and saw him look at me in surprise and I wondered if he thought me a very unnatural child because I did not cry. I felt nothing at all. I was just a blank, with no thoughts of any kind, any more than an empty balloon has thoughts.

"No more you are, ducks, but it's the ones that don't blare, that feels it the worst, in my experience."

Mrs. Higgins panted into the room wheezing like a barrel organ and the tears were streaming down her bluish face. The bottom part of her nose was flapping a bit as she fought for her breath. Her fat shoulders were back like a boxer's and her eyes stared a little, even through the tears. You could see the battle, she fought for air in the way her neck and the top of her chest moved in and out.

"Oh, B'linda!" she gasped. "What did you . . . want to run up here . . . like that for?"

She sat down on a chair suddenly.

"You didn't ought to have . . . seen your Mum . . . not like that . . . all sudden."

The policeman put me down beside her and I laid my hand on her shoulder and told her that I was sorry that her asthma was so bad.

"I'll run and get your asthma pump for you if you like," I offered politely, for it was a job I was quite used to doing for her. She never seemed to have it, when it was necessary. I think she was touched by my thoughtfulness for her, even in my own trouble, although I was acting like a mechanical doll with no feelings at all. She put her head down on her arms on the table and she wept at my suggestion and I looked up at the policemen and saw that they were worried about her. They had probably never seen a woman with bad asthma and I was used to seeing poor Mrs. Higgins like it.

"It's usually on her sitting-room mantelpiece," I said. "Do you think I might go and fetch it for her? It always makes her well very quickly."

One of the men went off to get it and the other looked at me as if he thought I was a strange child. I asked him what had happened to Mother.

"Heart attack," he told me. "Mother Higgins found her on the couch like she lays now. Doctor said it was sudden and that she wasn't long gone. It was peaceful too, so he said. There wasn't nothing nobody could have done, if they were here."

"There wasn't nothing nobody could have done," I thought. It was not the least bit right. Our English mistress would have been cross about it. I stayed there up near the ceiling and thought to myself. "There was nothing anybody could have done. There was not anything anybody could have done. There was nothing to be done. Nobody could have done anything."

"There wasn't nothing nobody could have done," he repeated in a kindly way, and I stood on the floor by his side and began to feel the first whispers of panic in my heart. Garry was right. He was always right . . . always. Mother was dead and gone and I would never talk to her again. I went to the mantelpiece and took down the blue envelope.

"There's a telegram in here," I told them. "It's to be sent off at once if anything happens. The money's ready inside and it's just right."

Mrs. Higgins lifted her head and looked interested and the other policeman came back and gave her her spray. "Whuff! Whuff! Whuff!" it went and then came her breath out wheezing, straining, whistling.

"I suppose we should open it up, Bert?"

The policeman was reading out the message.

"Sutherland, Old Jethart, Innish, Argyll, Scotland. Mary Stuart died today. Collect bequest with undying love."

"I don't get this at all, Bert," he said, scratching his head. "How did she know she was going to be dead today? Who is this sent to anyway?"

Mrs. Higgins talked to him between gasps and pumpings.

"She was very ill . . . doctor told her . . . the last time . . . only gave her a few months. She was off her head . . . about the kid. I don't blame her."

"And who's this Sutherland?"

"I don't know . . . never said ought about a Sutherland. Kept herself to herself . . . good neighbour though . . . always ready to lend a cuppa flour . . . cuppa sugar . . . when she had it herself . . . but dressmaking . . . don't pay nuthing these days. A few bob here . . . a few bob there . . . there's no money in it to keep . . . body and soul . . . together. She was a good poor thing . . . may Jesus receive her . . . sweet soul."

The cold feeling was beginning to come into my breast like heavy ice. Mrs. Higgins put her arms about me and hugged me to her fat breasts and I felt strongly comforted at the familiar dirty smell of her body. I was very glad of her kindness and sympathy.

"Don't worry, ducks," she wept. "Higgins won't see you put in no orphanage. You can come downstairs and live with us. We'll foster you, like our own little gel." She wiped her eyes in a grey-looking bit of rag and tried to smile at me.

"Since Glad married and went off up North, Higgins and me has been that lonely. Don't fret now. You'd like to come downstairs and live with your Auntie Higgins, wouldn't you?"

The doctor was in the room, but I had not noticed him coming in. I heard him talking to the constables. He said that there would be no need for a P.M. or an inquest, but I did not know what that meant.

"Mitral incompetence," he said, "Death from natural causes."

He had the telegram form in his hand and he put his arm on my shoulder and drew me away from Mrs. Higgins. He sat down on a chair and he put me between his two knees.

"Do you happen to know about this, Belinda?" he asked me and I nodded my head.

"Who was it addressed to, my dear?" he said. "Do you know?"

"It's to Cousin David." I told him.

"And who is Cousin David?"

"He lives in Scotland and his farm is called Old Jethart and he's to take me away . . not tomorrow, but perhaps the next day. I'm to live in his house with him and be looked after for the rest of my life. He knew all about it and he'll come at once. You can rely on him and not be frightened that he won't come. I've been left to him in Mother's will."

There was surprise at this, as well there might be and he put up a finger to touch my cheek.

"I'll get this wire off at once then, but first I'll see if there's a phone number. If there is, I'll ring him, explain what's happened."

He smiled at me, putting back my hair from my face.

"He'll come as quickly as he can. Be sure of that. He's a lucky chap. I'd come like lightning, if somebody had been kind enough to leave me a girl like you."

Later on, he gave me a small white pill and told me it would make me sleep, when I thought I might never sleep again as long as I lived. Then he fixed it all up with Mrs. Higgins.

"I take it she can stay with you for the present? We'll have the patient shifted to the hospital straight away."

I went to the door with Mrs. Higgins, but I stopped on the landing and wondered if I should go back and kiss Mother goodbye. Mrs. Higgins put her arm about my shoulders and told me not to worry. She said I could see her in the hospital chapel, when the women had washed her and tidied her up a little. I sat in Mrs. Higgins' parlour and wished I knew who the 'women' were, who did this awful work and Garry said that they would put a white nightdress on Mother and lay her on a table in the room at the hospital, where all the dead people lay, with their toes stuck up in a horrible way under the white sheets that covered them. I pushed the thought into the back of my mind and took a drink of the hot cocoa, which Mrs. Higgins had given me and I felt the room mist around me. She puffed upstairs to fetch my nightdress from under my pillow and then she waited while I undressed and got in the feather bed. She sat down beside me, still puffing from the exertion of the climb.

"Is Mother still up there?" I asked.

"You don't want to worry your head over things like that." she said, her voice deep and hoarse. "They've taken her. Linkman's the Undertakers . . . do it all ever so nice, ducks . . . In a day or two, we'll go to the Chapel o' Rest and you can see her as she lays in her coffin taking her last sleep."

Her words packed more solid ice into my chest, but the pill was making me feel hazy. A tear rolled down my cheek and Mrs. Higgins put her arms about me. I could hear the whuff-

whuff of her breathing against my ear and it was strangely lulling and soothing. On the edge of sleep, I dreamt that Mother was there, holding me tightly and again I thought I heard her light, sweet voice...

"I had a little nut tree, nothing would it bear,

But a silver nutmeg and a golden pear..."

I closed my eyes and felt the tears flow freely, turned my face against Garry-monkey's yellow jumper, willed the thoughts to him.

"We'll see Old Jethart. Cousin David will soon be here. He'll love us like she loved us. We'll see the white gate, the river, the stepping stones, the mountains with snow on their heads".

No matter how tightly I closed my eyes, I could see his boot-button-black gaze and hear his answer.

"We'll see them, but she won't, not ever again in this world. She'll never sing that song again . . . never . . . never . . ."

I slept deeply and woke up the next morning and forgot what had happened and remembered it, felt the shock fresh again. I was standing in my bodice and knickers by the bed, wondering where to wash, when Mrs. Higgins came in.

"Good morning, B'linda and good news too! The doctor brung round a message for you . . . said that he'd spoken to Mr. Sutherland. You'll be welcome in Old-What's-its-Name, a wild outlandish place it sounds. He can't get here till tomorrow morning. It takes two days or thereabouts. It's all fixed beautiful. You're to go up to Scotland by London, the day of your mum's funeral..."

I stood and washed myself as best as I could at the kitchen sink and thought how different our rooms upstairs were from the Higgins' flat. They had a newspaper on the table and it had rings, where the milk bottle had been, and the tea-pot. A brown map of England marked where gravy had been spilt. Mother had done wonders to keep our home a cheerful place. There had been my patchwork quilt and the bright rag rugs, the yellow cretonne curtains. The Higgins had no curtains, only a piece of ragged net on a drooping wire. We were lucky, Garry-monkey and I, to have had Mother to look after us. It was going to be lonely without her. I felt as if I was rushing down on a giant swing when I thought of it, threw some cold water on my face to stop myself crying again. Then I finished dressing and sat down to breakfast. Mrs. Higgins and I had bread and margarine and hot, strong, scalding tea. Mr. Higgins had a boiled egg too and a slice of fried bread, because he went out to work and had to keep his strength up. I helped pack his sandwiches for lunch-time, thick wedges of bread and bloater paste. We emptied the last of the tea into an old squash bottle and put six spoons of sugar and a dash of milk into it, packed the lot into his haversack. The paste was finished and Mrs. Higgins asked what he would like the next day for a change. He took me to sit on the sofa with him and told me he was going to miss me when I was gone, that I was a "great little old girl."

"I'd like sardine spread tomorrow, if you're going to get su'thing different. I'm partial to that, mate."

They were very kind to me and I knew that I would miss them more than they missed me. When Mr. Higgins had gone off to work, I cleared the table and washed up, spread some fresh newspaper as a table cloth. Mrs. Higgins was pleased with me, especially when I asked her if I could help tidy up. She told me where the brush was and watched me proudly, as I failed to make much difference to the confusion. For all the poverty, it was a home and they were very kind to me, although the doctor did not approve of their idea about what was proper behaviour in bereavement. He came in later on and put me standing between his knees again, while he took off one of my bows and re-tied it neatly.

"In two days, you'll be in Scotland, Belinda. What plans have you for today?"

Mrs. Higgins turned off the wireless and her voice was confidential and lowered in respect.

"I've to take her down to see her mum. She'll be coffined by now, if the funeral's tomorrow and she'll be looking lovely. Then we'll go down town and buy a black dress. This cousin from Sotland will want to see her in mourning at the funeral and that's only fittin'."

The doctor looked at me and then his eyes took in the room, the bare dirty floor-boards, the torn curtains, the piece of liver from the butcher's, lying on the window-sill to be dropped into the pan for supper tonight.

"It's not advisable for the child to go to see . . . to see . . . nor attend the funeral, nor be decked out in black at her time of life."

Mrs. Higgins was put out at him for that.

"Well, it don't show much respect to the dead, I'm sure," she said huffily and I picked Garry-monkey up from the sofa and clutched him close to my chest.

"It's her guardian's orders. He won't have her emotions paraded for a peep-show. The less she has to do with death the better. I agree with him and you'd best see to it that what he wants is done."

I spent a miserable day after that, for Mrs. Higgins was inclined to be disapproving of me. She was disgusted at the thought of me walking round without proper decent black. It was a nice thing that a girl wasn't to be allowed to kiss her mum goodbye. She'd be looking ever so lovely in her coffin and the undertaker would have a pretty frill round her face, like might be in a chocolate box.

"It's nought to be afraid of, love."

I had no wish to go through the parade of death. I was relieved that I had not to go to the Chapel of Rest. If I saw Mother in her coffin with a frill round her face, I would scream and scream and never be able to stop. I think she thought me an un-natural child. Maybe Garry backed her up, but I told him it was because I loved Mother more and not less.

Then the day was over and the night coming down. Even in the company of the Higginses, with the wireless full on and the smell of frying liver filling the flat, even with the kind way they treated me and the jokes they made and the love they gave me, a great loneliness took possession of me. I was tired out, so they sent me off to bed and Mrs. Higgins came and tucked me up and talked to me. Mercifully, I slept deeply and the night was gone and breakfast was over and there was packing to be done, my best dress and coat to be put on. Mr. and Mrs. Higgins had a cup of tea before they left for the funeral. Then she kissed me and held me in her arms a long time, before she wheezed off down the stairs to the taxi. I watched them go and then I went back upstairs to the flat, with Garry tucked tightly against my breast. I must not start to cry. Cousin David would think me ungrateful indeed, if my eyes were red and miserable. The best thing was to busy myself to pass the time till they came back from the funeral. Cousin David would be there as well and presumably he would come home with them to collect me.

There was the packing to check. I opened the lid of Mother's case and counted the clean vests and knickers and bodices, two of each . . . hankies, Bible, Hymn-book, Prayer-book. Garry muttered to me that Mother might be sad, because I had not gone with the others. It might be a good thing to find the place in the Prayer-book and try to follow the service. The Order for the Burial of the Dead . . . the small print, I could not understand some of it, except the part about the Priests and the Clerks meeting the Corpse at the entrance of the Churchyard and all in capital letters.

"I am the resurrection and the life, saith the Lord . . ."

I read on slowly, my mind shying like a frightened horse from the Garry-monkey thoughts. The twenty third psalm was an old friend, waiting in the darkness to take my hand. I knelt at the bed and said it over, as I had so often said it with her, but it was soon finished and I was back with the hard reality of the burial service. I could not go on with it. I closed the book, packed it away, went over to the window and lifted my eyes to the grey of the sky.

"Please, God, hold her warmly in your everlasting arms. Let her be safe under your feathers. Guard and keep her for ever, for Jesus' sake. Don't let her miss me at the grave-side. It wasn't because I didn't love her, God . . ."

Back at the case, there was more packing to check . . . the shiny gaberdine mack, my skirt and the jumper, she had knitted, two white blouses, two face towels, a bath towel . . .

I wanted to take the patchwork quilt, but there was no room for it. Cousin David might know if I could have it sent on, but suddenly I was sick of heart and turned away.

It was cold in the flat, for the money had run out in the meter and I had no more to put in. The fire was out and the gas off. I put on my blue Harris tweed overcoat and my straw boater that had a blue ribbon to match. Mother had made the coat the winter before and it had a red silk lining from an old dress. She had turned out her scanty wardrobe to find something and the dress had made a cloak of grandeur out of a plain Harris tweed coat. We had had a great triumph with it. This year, only this year, she had let down the hem. I ran my finger over the tiny stitches and remembered how skilfully she had done it, not three months past.

"Of course, you can't see where it's been turned down, honey. You're not supposed to."

The hat was too summery, but it was the only one I possessed, so I had no choice but to wear it . . . and now it was time to finish the packing and close the case and close a chapter of my life. Last of all, I put in the book of poems from the table at Mother's side of the bed, snapped the lid shut. Garry-monkey was watching my face to see if I cried, so I picked him up and went back to the window, with his face soft against my neck and the crew-cut stubbling my chin. There was a restlessness and loneliness and an emptiness, that was unbearable. Out on the landing, I looked into the street. The Higgins' taxi should soon bring them back and a taxi was a rare sight in the neighbourhood. I waited a long time, till I began to wonder if they would ever come back.

Then I heard a car coming along the street, looked out and saw it was a taxi, going slowly and hesitantly past the houses, as if the driver was searching for an address. It stopped below my high window and a man in a dark suit got out, paid the driver, stood with his back to the road, looking up at the house, then down at the three shallow steps. His hand touched the iron railings that skirted the steps, ran along the curved metal part of it that was worn and polished from generations of hands. So he disappeared through the front door and I knew it must be Cousin David and my heart tapped at my ribs. I looked over the banisters and could see him coming up the stairs and the way his hand travelled the rail of the banisters still. As he reached the landing below, I stepped back to the window and faced the place he must appear and the blood had run from my face, leaving me like a wax doll. Then he was round the turn of the last flight and coming on towards me, stopping up short as he saw me, then coming on more slowly as if he was trying to catch a butterfly and did not want to frighten it away. On the landing he paused again, white-faced too and with a hunger in his eyes, taking in every detail of me, the white socks, the tweed coat, the ribbon bows, the straw boater. I gripped Garry-monkey more tightly still and his crew-cut ground comfort into my chin, as I held out my right hand and tried to remember what the polite thing was to say.

"You'll be Mr. David Sutherland, of Old Jethart, Innish, Argyll?"

He looked at me helplessly and then took my hand in his and made me a small bow.

"You'll be Mistress Belinda McLean then. I don't think you'll ever know what it means to me to see you."

We were very formal with each other. There was an awkwardness, as if we were complete strangers, when, of course, he was as familiar to me as if I had known him for years. He was taller than I had thought him and his hair was flecked with silver. My imagination had crayoned him in the kilt, but he wore a dark grey suit and a black tie, which made him seem white-faced.

"Would you like to come in?"

It would be polite to show him the flat, but I fretted because the gas was all gone. It was cold and there was no hospitality I could offer him. In Scotland, he would be offered tea, shortbread, a Selkirk bannock, maybe hot scones with butter running out of them. Did I not know it well, as well as I knew the white gate and the silver river? I had no money for the gasmeter and worse than that, I had no milk. There was some in Mrs. Higgins' kitchen, but I could not go and borrow it without asking her.

In the living room, he stood with his back to the fireplace, his searching glance taking in the whole scene. I had made the place as tidy as possible, but it was dead without her. There was no sense to the work-box and the sewing machine, the knitting pins, with the brown wool cast on and the first few rows of Garry-monkey's new jumper.

Very slowly, he walked about the room, going to the window to look out, scanning the scrubbed white of the kitchen table, kicking his shoe into the thickness of the rag rugs, examining the butter-box-seat, lifting a blue cup and fitting it to its saucer. I felt worse than ever because I had nothing to offer him, blamed myself for not arranging something beforehand with Mrs. Higgins. Maybe I could fix something with her belatedly? She might have come home by now.

"Would you like some tea?"

"No . . . no . . . no . . ."

He seemed to have forgotten that I was there, just went off to the bedroom and I trailed along behind him, like a small ghost. The brass bedstead with the patchwork quilt held his attention, far more than I did. He lifted the edge of the coverlet and murmured to himself that she would have made it, opened the lid of the packed case and saw the book of poems, which lay on top of the clothes. It might have been a snake with the way he shut the case fast on it. His face twisted in a grimace of pain and he was at the window in a stride, looking out across the landscape of grey slate roofs.

"Have you still got Lady Gay?" I asked him to try to break up the desolation of the empty room, for empty it was, for all that we still inhabited it.

He turned round and his face was in shadow. It cost him a mighty effort to drag himself back to the present. I could see he was wondering who Lady Gay might be and how she came into the situation. Then suddenly he knew what I was talking about, but there was a puzzlement in his face how I could know anything about Lady Gay.

"Mother told me about her," I explained. "She was always talking about Old Jethart. You'd be surprised at all I know. It started off as a kind of bedtime story. When I was small, she used to tell it to me before I went to sleep . . . about how she would ride in along the mountain road and about the special catch on the white gate . . . and the twist of the avenue and the trees and the way you could look down at the river . . . and the stepping-stone place . . . and the house on the hill. It's very good of you to take me to live there. I haven't even said 'thank you', and I haven't given you any hospitality. I did ask if you'd like a cup of tea, but I'd better tell you that I've got no money for the gas and there's no milk. Mrs. Higgins took Mother's bag..."

I wondered if Cousin David was ill, for his face was as white as death and I could hardly bear the pain in his eyes.

"Lady Gay?" he said, and there was a soft Scots burr to his voice. "No, I haven't Lady Gay now, but don't fret yourself about that. I was thinking it over, since I got your letter. Thank you for your letter. It was a pity it came too late, but that wasn't your fault. Still, I was thinking over Lady Gay on the journey down. I've got another mare as like her as two peas in a pod. She's a hand smaller, but that's all to the good."

He seemed more happy in himself to talk about the horses, for he had lost the white pain and he was smiling a little.

"The pony, she's called 'Judy'. Maybe we'll call her 'Lady Judy' and she'll be yours. Can you ride?"

"I've never actually ridden, but I know how to."

He laughed outright at that and told me there was a vast difference between theory and practice and I quenched the laughter for him and did not know why, when I told him that Mother had taught me all about riding, how you must be part of the horse and keep your hands and your heels down, and how you must never leave the white gate open, in case the stock strayed out on the mountain road. He snapped the locks on the case shut and lifted it, looked round the room for the last time, as if he meant to photograph it on his mind.

"I've fixed with the people downstairs to have anything you want sent on."

I ran my finger along the small stitches of the patchwork quilt.

"I'd not like to leave the quilt and of course, I'll take Garry-monkey. I have him here."

"Garry-monkey?" he said. "Oh, yes, I see."

He put down the case near the door and came back to the bed, began to fold up the patchwork quilt and in the dim light

40

it made a glory of colour as it always did. I put Garry-monkey down on a chair and I helped him with the folds. He tucked the roll of quilt under his arm, never bothered about wrapping paper and I was glad of this, for I had none. In two strides, he was at the door picking up the case, looking round the room again.

"Don't forget yon animal," he reminded me and there was a ghost of a smile to me, as I hugged Garry-monkey tight to my chest and rubbed my chin against the crew-cut, for he wore his wool hat on the back of his head and there was a line of hair along the front of his brow, that was rough to the touch. I took off the cap and showed the hair-cut to Cousin David.

"When I was five and he was four, I borrowed Mother's scissors and cut his hair. I thought it would grow again in a week or two, was sad when it didn't. I was only young at the time..."

"Well, put the creature's cap on again and let's go."

I set the yellow wool cap at its jaunty angle and turned round so that Garry could have a last look at the room too. Then my hand was in his and we were going down the stairs. At the Higgins's door I paused, but he told me they were not at home. The taxi had come back for him. He must have arranged it beforehand, but there it was, with the man getting out to take the case. I turned to look up at the house. Side by side, Cousin David and I, we stood there and looked up at the dirty bricks and the cracked window panes. Right at the top, there was a flash of bright colour and I remembered the way Mother had made the curtains to bring sunshine into the room. She had succeeded too...

Cousin David opened the taxi door and got in beside me, leaned over and told the driver to take us to the Station Hotel.

"Did you have any porridge to your breakfast?" he asked me and I shook my head and said that I had not been hungry.

The car moved off along the street and I watched the familiar houses glide past like figures on a moving belt. There was the post-box, there was the grocer's and last of all the school. Now, we were speeding up, like guests coming home from a funeral and the houses were strange houses and the shops strange shops.

"I had no time to take breakfast myself, Mistress Belinda. It's past lunch-time and maybe it would be best if we stopped off at the hotel for a bite to eat?"

I was very hungry indeed, very surprised to find myself so. I had thought it likely that I might never be hungry again.

"I'd like it fine," I told him.

We stowed the case in the head-porter's cubby-hole, but Cousin David kept the quilt under his arm. I went off to the lady's room and came back to find him in the front hall, looking at the revolving doors. I didn't know it then, but I know it now, that there was a strange thought running through his head. There was a mystery about me and he knew it well, though I was only to find it out over the years. So David Sutherland was standing in the hall of an indifferent hotel far south of Old Jethart and the white gate with the latch that was convenient for the horseman passing by.

"So all I've got out of my life is this wee lassie and a patchwork quilt and a Garry-monkey . . . and that's a fine sum total if you put it down and draw a line under it . . . and say that's the end of it."

PART TWO

The Royal Scot was not due out of King's Cross till late at night. Cousin David told me that he had two sleepers booked on it, but I was not sure what that meant and I did not like to ask him. We had lunch soon after we quitted the flat and afterwards went by train to London. We left my case in the luggage office at King's Cross, but there was a long wait till the train left for Scotland and I was tired. He looked at my face helplessly and I knew he was wondering what to do with me in the interval. At last, he flagged a taxi and took me to a West End cinema, told me that it was the best place available for me to have a sleep. He promised to tell me the story over dinner, put his arm about me. I tried to stay awake, but there was a boring News-Reel. I knew it could be in no way right for me to attend a cinema when my mother was dead. I closed my eyes and remembered the flat and the long row of decrepit houses, wondered if they would be as lonely after me as I was after them . . . and was asleep. It was dark when we left the cinema. I was still half asleep, still half in the old life and half in the new. It was impossible that I should be in London with Cousin David and that he was taking me to dine very grandly in a restaurant nearby. I was not dressed properly for such an occasion, but I was past worrying about it.

"You'll no doubt want to go to the Ladies' Room. I'll meet you in the hall as soon as you're through."

Before I had taken three steps away from him, he called me back and looked more helpless than ever. I might want to tip the attendant. It was usual in such places. He shoved a handful of silver and pence into my hand and ran his hand through his hair as if he wished he was anywhere else but where he was.

I was awed at the palace quality of the hotel, and the cloak room was a queen's boudoir. There seemed a great many people there, reflecting back at themselves from an echelon of mirrors and hand basins. They were all intent on making up their faces and combing their hair, washing their hands. I was enclosed in a warm incense of pared-pencil, spiced, flower atmosphere, but I did not belong there and well I knew it. I stood over by the door, very alone and very small. The attendant came to see what I wanted, took me across to a tiled table, that had a saucer on it, with a few coins. It was a great relief that I had money in my pocket. My fingers explored to make sure it was still there.

"And where have you come from, Alice-in-Wonderland?"

I filled her in with my background, as best I could and she took Garry-monkey from me and removed his cap to look at his crew-cut. Then she left me and went to the door, peered along the corridor to see Cousin David.

"I'll slip and tell him that you'll be delayed a wee. I'd best see to that hair of yours, if you're going to dine wi' such a grand gentleman, for this is a very fashionable place."

I was attracting too much attention. First one lady and then another came to talk to me, as I sat in front of a mirror with the attendant combing my hair. Soon there were six, then seven, then eight, all whispering among themselves, and talking to me about Scotland and the trip to the north. I suppose they were like ewes in the fields that will take to a motherless lamb. I know it now, but that day, I was amazed at the kindness of so many strangers. It seemed a weird dream and presently I might wake up and be happy again and Mother would not be dead after all and there would be the kettle to put on to boil for breakfast. They tried my plaits in different styles and even put them up in a crown on my head. At last, they decided to double each plait back on itself and set a fresh bow at each ear. I was unhappy about the straw hat, but they were united in admiration for it. It went so well with the tweed coat and blue was the "in" colour. Still it might be best to carry it, so that people could see my hair style. We took so long about it, that I fretted that Cousin David might get impatient and go without me. The attendant went to reassure him and very soon I was ready. I was frightened of the grandeur of the establishment for I had never been in such a place before and I hoped that I might know what was good manners to do.

My heart failed me before the dining room doors, for they had an Arabian Night look to them. A man in a swallow-tailed coat came sailing down between the tables to greet us, his hand held out in welcome. I took it in mine, for I thought he meant to shake hands, but it seemed I had made a mistake.

Still he was not put out with me, just put his arm about my shoulder and took us to a table, pulled out a chair for me and handed me the menu. He beckoned imperiously and in no time at all we had a wine waiter and an ordinary waiter and all of them very anxious about what we might like to eat. The head waiter was a person of great importance. He took Garry-monkey and sat him in a chair by himself and told me that my "bambino" was "multo bello". The wine waiter was interested in Garry's crew-cut and said it was a good thing the hair had not grown. He came from Italy himself and the crew cut was high fashion like in the States. He thought that maybe the still lemonade might be the best thing for me to drink. The ordinary waiter advised me to start with melon. It was very good tonight, they all agreed. It was like a ship and it sailed on green ice. The mast was a cocktail stick and the sail a piece of white card.

Cousin David sat and said nothing, just looked at me as if he had never seen a child before in his life and as if he had no more idea what to do with me than if I had been a chimpanzee like Garry come alive. I was still in a mist of unreality and unhappiness, wanting nothing so much as to be in my own bed again.

The room was immense and there were tables lined up as far as the eye could see, an orchestra on a high place. There were waiters in dark coats, some pushing trolleys, some carrying plates or glasses or wine or coffee or knives and forks or just nothing at all. The menus were produced with a special flourish at the tables and the linen was snow white.

The head waiter was from Italy too and he had a little girl just about my age and how old was I? He took out his pocketbook and showed me her picture, dark, with eyes like sloes and her name was Maria. Best of all, she liked a small piece of Sole with Sauce Tartare . . . and perhaps Chicken Vol-au-vent to follow. For a special treat, she might care for Crêpes suzettes. As this was my first night in London and I was obviously going to take the town by storm, he advised the Crêpes suzettes. I was in a maze of sounds and voices, the clinking of cutlery, the hum of talking. The orchestra was trying out snatches of tune, as if they spread samples of their talent for us to pick and choose. I was all confusion, doubt and fear and could only sit and try to remember my manners. The array of knives and forks alarmed me, but the ordinary waiter took them all away and put them back in pairs, as the time to use them came, and that made it easy. I remembered to thank them and exclaimed in delight at the exciting things. I had never thought to inhabit such a world and I hoped that I might not shame Cousin David by my ignorance. He passed the time by telling me about the story of the picture which he had seen while I slept. I was sorry to have missed it because it was a Walt Disney, but Cousin David said that the sleep had done me better than Mickey Mouse and maybe we would see it again, when it came to Innish in a hundred years time. We laughed about that but it was thin laughter, I wondered if it were wrong for a girl to laugh on the day of her mother's funeral. There was a sympathy between us. I had sensed it in the flat and again a dozen times during the day. He seemed to know what I was thinking as soon as I thought it.

"Mary Stuart wid na wish you greet for her because she was gane awa'." he said leaning close to me, his voice very Scots and thick with emotion, his eyes soft with pity, drenched with sadness. "She was never done laughing and you've got the same way wi' you . . . the same way you hold your heid, the dark green een, the same white smile . . ."

The lady from the cloakroom had appeared at the door, has whispered to the doorman and the doorman had whispered to the headwaiter and the headwaiter had whispered to the leader of the band. I saw it all happen as I flaked the pastry of the vol-au-vent with my fork, the same way Cousin David did it.

It was impossible that the conductor should be bowing in my direction, that every member of the band should be smiling. Then they gave us "Over the Sea to Skye" and "Highland Laddie" and "Will ye no Come back again?" and a dozen more, songs that she had sung me many a time, and they did not know what they did to my composure. When they had finished, they stood and bowed to me and I smiled at them and managed not to disgrace us by weeping. The only thing that stopped my total dishonour was the bursting into flame of the Crêpes and that turned my thoughts into a new channel and so lightened the quick sadness of childhood.

Then came the excitement of King's Cross, with a station as big as a town and people like ants, that scurried or crawled slowly to pass the time, or met and kissed or parted and kissed. There were porters in charge of rumbling trolleys of luggage and book stalls and bars and waiting rooms and parcels offices and all the time great trains, which crept out silently and smoothly as if they were snakes sliding out on their bellies like the serpent in the Garden of Eden. There were lines of red post vans with canvas sacks of letters and parcels. I wondered if my letter had travelled up to Scotland in such a way. Then we were past the porter at the Meccano gate and walking along the carriages of the Royal Scot.

I was to have a compartment to myself with a bunk bed in it and a basin and lights and a mirror. I unpacked my nightdress and dressing gown and Cousin David left me to it and went off, so that I was alone and terrified that I might never see him again, in this great echoing new world, that was full of the activity of trains that slid out and trains that slid in.

Then he was back again and only just in time, to my way of thinking. The train started ten minutes afterwards and I wondered what would have happened to me if it had gone off early. We were sliding out through a network of rails and over a jolting of points, past the lozenges of windows and the overhead lines of streets, on past factories and shops and sidings and stopped trains and bridges and tunnels and clankings and hissings and the smell of railways. I had got ready for bed and he tucked me up and hoped that I might not get indigestion from my late dinner.

"I'm next door. If you can't sleep bang on the wall. I'll be glad of your company. I never sleep on trains."

I thanked him for all he had done and he was awkward about it, wondered if he should kiss me good-night and decided against it . . . then changed his mind and bent his head to kiss my cheek and so took himself off.

I lay in the dimness and the train went flying through the night with the wheels singing their song.

"Innish, Argyll . . . Innish, Argyll, Innish, Argyll . . . Old Jethart, Old Jethart, Old Jethart, Old Jethart . . . Innish, Argyll, Innish Argyll, Innish Argyll . . ."

I woke up hours later and it was still dark when I looked

through the window. Back in the safety of my warm bed, I gathered Garry-monkey close and knew it was long past the time, when I should stop putting my black thoughts in his head. The black thoughts were my own, now every minute that passed, the train was carrying me farther away from my old home . . . Mother's grave would be under the darkness and the loneliness of the black velvet sky with maybe the stars like pin diamonds overhead. There would be nobody to tend it, nobody to care. I turned my face into Garry's yellow sweater and felt the old pain heavy in the roots of my tongue. The afternoon and evening had been a dream of riches . . . a nightmare. Cousin David had been a kind stranger. They had all conspired to help me on my way, so many kind strangers, but I wanted Mother alive again. I pictured her face, the dimple on her chin, the way she would say "Don't fret, honey." I could hear her say it as if she sat on my bunk with her hand stretched out to stroke my hair.

There was no sound as the door opened, only a light from the corridor that dimmed my faint light to nothing. Then the door slid closed again and a hand was on my face and the dim light had come into its own again. Cousin David sat down on the edge of the bunk and tucked Garry-monkey more comfortably against my neck.

"I wasn't alseep either. I was minding the day your Mother came to Old Jethart. Would you wish I would tell you about it?"

My hand was in his and his voice was full of dreams.

"It goes back a long way. My mother was gone and your Aunt Con came over from Ireland to keep house for us . . . my father and me. She brought the light back to Old Jethart. It had been miserable. Then your mother came visiting Con . . ."

I took up the story from him, for I knew it well, or thought I did, but I had not got one fifth of it.

"She went to Dublin, to a place called the North Wall. It was on the River Liffey. She crossed to Greenock and it was very rough. The Stewardess told her she was a good sailor . . . and she passed Ailsa Craig where they make stones for curling. Then she got a train and came to Argyll and it was still three miles to go from the station and you met her in a trap with a pony . . ."

He reminded me wryly that he was supposed to do the telling.

"What was she like when she was young?" I asked him.

He told me that Mother had never been old.

"She was ower young tae dee."

He was away in some secret land of his own, back in the past.

"She was very like your Aunt Con . . . like as two peas in a pod they were, but she was gay. She was always laughing . . . walked as if she were dancing a foot above the ground with her head in the sunshine. She was a bonnie, bonnie lassie."

There was a long silence and I wondered if he had gone to sleep, but after a while he went on and the train sang a background to the words with its "Innish, Argyll, Innish Argyll."

"I met her at the station with the trap, like you said, thought she'd be dead-beat with the journey, but she was sparkling with excitement. Nothing would do but for her to take the reins. Con told her not to be so daft, told her that the pony was a wild one and to leave me to do the driving. "No pony ever got the better of me," she laughed, so I let her have her way. Then Con told her it was a good thing it was fine weather and that there was nobody to put up an umbrella in the trap, for the pony could never abide an umbrella. She was annoyed about the whole thing. She was a serious sort of lassie. Your mother looked across at me and dared me to put up the umbrella . . . and I did . . . and we were off in a flash. She stopped him a mile along the road and Con not talking to either of us . . and she winked at me . . . and so we came to Old Jethart . . ."

I woke up later on when the train had sighed to a stop in Edinburgh and never remembered when I went asleep. There was washing and dressing to be done in a small space. Edinburgh was a strange aroma . . . soft lilting voices . . . a gentleness and a slowing down of time . . . a warm friendliness. We had breakfast in the hotel at the Station and then we walked the length of Prince's Street. We had shopping to do and I was awed by the splendour of the shops. We had to buy riding kit, jodhpurs, yellow sweaters with polo necks, yellow string gloves, a tweed hacking jacket with slits at the back, a black velvet jockey cap, the last so that I did not crack my skull the moment I arrived in Argyll. It was time I had a party dress, Cousin David said, and he set the lady in the shop to find one to our tastes. I shall never forget that dress, if I live to be the age of one hundred and ten. It was in crimson velvet, with a hand-made lace collar, very full in the skirt . . . a high ruched waist. I liked the riding kit better and could hardly bear to exchange it for my blue tweed coat and straw boater. I was pleased beyond anything when Cousin David told me to keep it on, so I walked at his side along the road to the Rock, dressed as I had never been dressed before, very proud of myself. We looked down upon Prince's Street, on the traffic that beetle-crawled, on the cars and lorries and the scarlet of bus after bus, after bus. Then we had to make a phone call to Old Jethart.

"There's somebody you'll meet there and it's time I told you about him . . . a lad called Hamish. I got him the way I got you . . . in a will, if you choose to put it like that."

He rang from the Hotel and I stood by his side, with my heart thumping my ribs at the thought that he was speaking to somebody in Old Jethart. He was ringing from Edinburgh because he had come through here to see to the audit. I did not know what he meant by that. Yes, he had me with him and we would soon be home. There was a static of voice at the other end of the line and I imagined the boy, who stood in the hall maybe, wondered if he were dark or fair, if he were much older than I was myself . . . how it came that he had been left in a will.

"I want you to meet us with the trap, Hamish."

That brought me back from my flights of fancy. There was some argument, but Cousin David was determined.

"Of course, the car would be the sane method of transport. There's a reason. I'll explain later on. I'm not out of my mind. It's very important. It's the way a particular lady must travel to Old Jethart, whether it's winter or high summer. Come snow or dark . . ."

Then . . . "Those lamps are about somewhere. Take a keek in the harness room."

At last, the conversation was at an end and the phone back in its socket. We walked up the hill of one of the side streets off Prince's Street and came to an office building that might have crept out of Bleak House. It was a charcoal house in a line of other charcoal houses and there were brass plates by the door. I waited in a room, while Cousin David went off along a corridor with an elderly man. After a while they came back and the man looked at me for a long time and said so I was Belinda and we shook hands and I hoped he was well. He told me he found the cold weather trying and that he thought it might snow later on. Then he smiled at me and took off my jockey cap to get a good look at me.

"I've got a strange idea in my head, David. I think this wee lassie walks in the sun, think maybe she'll bring good luck to Old Jethart in the end of it. It's way past the time for good luck . . . and it's almost way past the time of your train."

In a flash, it seemed, we were in the train, with the city falling away from all around us and the country opening up. I had never seen actual mountains, but now from the carriage windows I saw them, snow-capped, mighty and mightier, range upon range. The lochs were slate that turned blue under the sun. The clouds chased their shadows as if they would outrun the train.

"How old is Hamish?"

"Older than you. I've had him for six years. He's my cousin's boy, but he's no blood kin to you. It was on the other side. He's dour and he's dark, but you'll get on fine with him when you know him. He's a good laddie."

The rivers were swollen with the winter and the water had taken possession of the hills. There were falls like skeins of wool, that matched the sheep's fleeces. The snow lay patchy in the fields and on the mountain sides, tablecloths set out to dry.

Even in the cold weather, it was a beautiful country and it was no wonder that Mother had fallen in love with it in Spring and Summer. I felt a lifting of my spirits and then a sudden guilt that I had left Mother lonely in the dark of a distant grave . . . I went to sit beside Cousin David and again he knew what I was thinking and put his arm around me.

"Will she be lonely after us?" I asked him and looked in his eyes for my answer, found utter loneliness there and thought I knew his sympathy for me, but that was not what filled his eyes with pain.

He asked me if I knew about cremation and I told him that I did.

He held me so tightly that it was uncomfortable and told me that we would talk about it now, for it was best to get it over.

"Her ashes will be sent to Scotland very soon. When it's Spring again and the wee lambs are out on the hills, I'll take them to that cowslip field she told you about, on the other side of the river. She'll come home to Old Jethart . . ."

I knew if I started to cry, I would never stop. I would put on the red shoes of weeping and never be able to take them off again. I had to thank him, for it had been wonderfully kind on his part to have known how I felt about leaving Mother alone so far away.

I got through the thanks with a stiff face and he brushed aside any kindness on his part with muttered words that I heard as a whisper through his chest wall, where my ear was pressed.

"Maybe I did it for my own peace of mind," I heard, or I thought he said, thought he must have liked her a lot . . . Then he spun the subject back to Hamish and I was full of questions again. It seemed that I would have more to do with Hamish than I would with himself. He would be busy about the farm but Hamish would see to my welfare . . . teach me how to ride and that sort of thing.

"He's tough. If you fall off, don't expect any pity. He'll put you up again in a second and if you fall off again, you'll be in his bad books. Did I tell you he was dour and dark? That means he has a deal of black books to put you in . . ."

I fell asleep and when I woke, he told me we were the best of the way home and by that he meant that we had not much longer to travel. The night was coming down around us and there were more and more snow table-cloths and soon whole fields of white. Now the mountains were pressing all about us, as if they wanted to creep in out of the cold and the darkness. He told me the names of some of them before the night spirited them away. There was a pewter lake, that winked at us in the light of the moon and he told me he fished there sometimes and so would I. Then he got to his feet and assembled the case and the parcels, for we were sliding into Innish Station.

"Welcome home, Belinda."

It was a single platform with white rails and a lamp that cast a circle of light. The snow on the platform boards was whiter than the railings. I pressed my face to the window and looked out but there was nobody there. It might have been a forgotten station in a dead world, for nothing moved except the sift of a few snow flakes. Then the train rattled and sighed to a halt, and Cousin David was on the platform with his hands stretched to me. Another moment and I was beside him, turning to walk at his side to a gate where another lamp held a cone of light. A man was collecting the tickets and a pony was tied to the railings . . . a black pony with a cloth over her back, and flakes of snow on her mane.

The porter looked at me with great curiosity, as Cousin David handed him the tickets.

"I've been to London, Jock, to fetch a wee lassie."

"Aye, aye. So this is Mistress McLean?"

The Scots knew how to pronounce my name and it made me feel that I had come home. "MacLane," they called it and it had a royal sound on their tongues that it did not possess in its toothpaste international version. I shook the porter's hand and said I was glad to meet him and that I hoped he was well and not feeling the cold of the night, for it was very cold indeed now and my words turned into white vapour, as soon as they left my lips.

"Mister Hamish has brought the pony and trap. It was a gey kind thought. I mind the time your mither came to this station and took the same trap doon the road in a gallop . . ."

He had a lantern in his hand and he held it up and looked in my face.

"She'll never be deid wi' you alive . . . your Aunt Con either."

There was a tall young man in the background . . . a man in a kilt . . . and Cousin David introduced him to me as Hamish. He took my hand in his and looked down at the yellow string gloves, took in the riding kit, asked me if I had ridden all the way and I thought that there was a sarcastic tone in his voice, but maybe I was wrong, for he was kind enough to have brought me sugar lumps for the pony, so that I might get into her favour.

"Belinda knows well how to hold the sugar on the palm of her hand," said Cousin David and there was a weariness about him after the long journey. "She has all the theory of horsemanship, but none of the practice yet."

The two lamps on the trap made a glory of the kilt, as Judy accepted the sugar and nuzzled into my pocket for more. Then she turned her head to watch me go round to the back of the governess trap to get in. I had been hearing about the trap for years, but it was completely unlike my mental picture. There was a smell of leather and pony and straw . . . straw to keep your feet warm, and a rug to wrap round your shoulders and a hot bottle for your lap, and a sky of stars. I was in front of Cousin David against the warmth of his side, choked with the grandeur of the equipage. We set off smartly along the road and the lamps shone sunshine on the snow. After a while the sky plucked geese and sent the feathers gently down on us and the frost glittered from the pine trees and there was a peace and a silence, except for the dull-rapping of the hooves. I settled Garry-monkey warmly against the hot bottle and remembered to thank Hamish for bringing it and the rug.

I called him Mr. Sutherland and he looked at me with suspicion, as if I had called him "Mr" for a joke.

"I'm Hamish," he said looking down at his bony knees and his kilt was subdued in the gloom of the night to a grey drab, that was no relation to what it had been in the lamp light. "Don't call me Mister Anything, Mistress McLean."

It was a long road but there was a magic in every inch of it. The trees were bent down as if there was a storm blowing. I asked Hamish why this was and he told me it was because of the prevailing winds. Then he saw that I did not understand what he meant and he unbent and explained that the wind blew almost always in the one direction and that it shaped the trees so.

"It's a pity that you came so late. You can't see the mountains, but they're all around us. This is a green valley in the spring."

The pony's hooves rang off-sharp against the hard frosted snow of the off-sharp road and the ice sparkled at us with millions of small brilliant eyes. Tiny waterfalls along the bank hung in silver icicles. Then there was a stone wall at one side and it was the start of Old Jethart land and after a long while, we were turning into the avenue. I looked at the white gates in the light from the trap lamps, with the grey stone walls running in to meet the big white pillars. I saw the latch that you used when you rode in on your horse and the tears trickled slowly down the cold of my cheeks, for it was like Christmas . . . and magic . . . holy and wonderful.

"There's your white gate, hinny."

Hamish threw the reins to Cousin David and got out to open the gate and soon we were driving under the trees along the avenue, that wound about to the house with the gate shut safe behind us. The river was there but the darkness mantled it. Then we were approaching the house. I knew we were climbing a grassy hill and when the snow cleared and the day came, I would see it. It seemed quite impossible that I was coming up the slope to Old Jethart. I hoped that they would not see I was crying, but Cousin David was wrapping me more tightly in the rug and it came to me that he had seen my tears. Hamish was sorry for me too, maybe because he knew what it was to be left to somebody in a will and to come driving up an avenue into a strange house. He tucked Garry-monkey more warmly against my side, leaned over to do it, tucked the rug about me right up to my neck, covered Garry-monkey completely in from the cold air.

"We'll soon be home, Belinda. I don't know if David has told you about Maggie. She and her daughter do the housekeeping. They knew your mother and your Auntie Con. They've been looking out the window all day, to see you coming . . . and the train not out of Edinburgh."

We turned round into a sweep of snow and the house was dark solid against the starlit sky with a wisp or two of cloud above its chimneys. It was far bigger than I had imagined it. The door was a rectangle of soft light, that shone out down the six steps. It was a proud, silent, challenging place, as if it faced out to the world and said "I have stood here for hundreds of years, and no man shall push me down."

At the foot of the steps was Maggie in a white apron, all granny-softness and grey hair and reaching arms. I had been wound up in a cocoon of rug and there was a moment to disentangle me and to restore Garry-monkey to his rightful place in my arms, for he got lost in the welter of rug. Then I was running like a leveret into Maggie's embrace and the tears frosted on my cheeks.

"Losh, hinny! You're so like your mither . . . the same wee turned-up nose, the smile, the bonnie green eyes, the black hair . . . like a raven's wing it was . . ."

Her daughter, May, was more matter of fact and she could see what her mother's words were doing to my composure. She led me up the steps into the hall, picked the cap off my head and hung it on the hall stand, exclaimed at my walking the streets of Edinburgh dressed in such a fashion.

"Have ye no sense in your head aboot what's right for town wear?" she scolded Cousin David and he put his arm on my shoulders and took me into the sitting room. There was an old man on his knees on the hearth-rug and if I had been a ghost, I could not have had more effect on him. He got to his feet with his bony hand held out to me, and the bright glow of the fire left him in shadow, for all the soft glow of the standard lamps.

"Ye've been awa' ower lang, Mistress."

The hairs on the nape of my neck prickled as I realised that he took me for my mother. The others were telling him who

I was and sweeping him away outside to unharness the pony.

"It's Mary Stuart's daughter."

He turned back to me from the door.

"If ye're yer mither's lass, ye'll be mistress of the hoose and sit at the foot of the table. It's high time ye cam' to Old Jethart. Our hairts are weary wi' waitin' for ye."

Maggie was telling us that my room was all ready. She would take me to it and bring me up hot water to wash. I was to change into a pretty dress and there was a fine supper waiting.

"I've given her the room that looks down over the river, the wee room, next your own, sir. You'll want her under your eye."

From somewhere, he produced the patchwork quilt, put it carefully into Maggie's hands. They had wrapped it up for us in Jenner's, and he undid it now.

"And that's to go on her bed. It's a very special quilt."

He poured himself a drink of whisky into a small glass and took it down in a gulp and I thought he looked more tired than anybody I had ever seen. I went over and took his hand in mine.

"It's lovely, Cousin David. It's a happy place, just as she said it was..."

Then Maggie had me by the shoulder and was leading me through the door and up the stairs to the most wonderful bedroom I had ever seen. There was a brass bedstead and May had the patch-work quilt on it in a flash and was exclaiming over the beauty of it. Then she had snapped my case open and was hanging my clothes in a brown wardrobe, that had small drawers all down one side of it. The dressing table had spindle legs and three mirrors and was elegant. Maggie had unwrapped the crimson velvet dress and I might have been a doll, with the way they dressed me up for my first supper in Old Jethart.

I went walking down the stairs by myself later on, for Maggie and May had gone on ahead "to see to the fowl." I crept down the staircase to the landing, turned and went on to the hall, heard voices from the sitting room, paused at the bottom step to listen.

"You're trying to re-capture a dream," said Hamish and the words had a bitter edge to them.

"No, it's not that . . ."

Cousin David's voice was softer and gentler and there was still a weariness in it.

"I can't explain it, Hamish. I've no way to tell you. It's getting stronger and stronger with every hour that passes, since I went up the stairs in that awful house. It was a slum, God knows, it was a slum, but she had made a home of it. I could feel her still there, when I had just seen her coffin . . ."

I had Garry-monkey under my arm and he whispered to me that there were coffins in Scotland too, and talk of coffins. I gave him a shake to change his thoughts and knew myself for a coward child.

"I haven't spoken much about it, laddie, but you're a man grown. You've seen what's gone on here these last years. Four days ago, it was ended, every last bit of a dream . . . every last hope of happiness. I had hoped, God knows I had hoped. I was in a grey world, with all brightness gone for aye. I don't remember much of the trip south. I try to put the funeral out of my head. There was nothing . . . nothing. I went up the stairs in the tenement and on the last landing a miracle happened. In the squalor, in the poverty, in the ruins of a man's happiness, in the dregs of my life, I saw her, a wee flower sprung from the ruins, as it happened in the bomb-scarred cities. She was in a blue coat . . . with a straw hat perched on her head in December, with a blue ribbon brave on it, to go with the coat. She was a forget-me-not, the one thing of beauty in the whole hideous house, in the whole hideous city. I got a feeling that it wasn't all lost. There was a flower plucked from disaster . . . She's quite some lassie. Stronger and stronger since I've been with her, I've had the thought that maybe it wasn't all a waste of time."

I could imagine Hamish's way of drawing down his black brows.

"In six-seven years, she'll be Mary Stuart come back again to walk Old Jethart. You'll be a middle-aged man by then. It's in my mind you'll break your heart."

I could not understand what they were talking about. There was something that I did not know . . . some mystery. There seemed no reason why Cousin David should break his heart about me, when I grew up, but now I thought that perhaps it was a joke, for they were laughing.

"I've got plans to wed her to you, Hamish. If you could get that black dog off your shoulder and smile a bit, you'd be a fine man for her. Old Jethart will be yours and hers when I'm gone. You could fill it with your bairns. It's a house that's waited over long for bairns."

The joke was on Cousin David's side, for Hamish was not amused.

"Don't waste your time match-making for me," he said crossly. "I don't like dark lassies . . . to much of the crow about them. When I'm good and ready, I'll find a fair-haired lass with eyes like the sea and a sweet way to her. I'm not waiting for yon prim little miss to grow up and marry me, so don't set your mind on it, for you'll only get let down again."

There was a sudden stop and a gasp and Hamish was apologising at something he had said, but still I could not understand what it was all about. I had listened and I had not heard well of myself finally, so I knew the proverb was true. Hamish thought I was a prim little miss. I had built up my self-esteem with Cousin David's description of his first sight of me, but really I knew the truth, even before Garry-monkey put it in my head.

"Don't think you were 'a thing of beauty' in that old winter coat and that old summer hat. Blue ribbon! Forget-me-not! You were a prim little miss and you're still a prim little miss. It wouldn't surprise me if you stay a prim little miss all your life, with the way you go on."

I looked at Garry's boot-button eyes and wondered how he got so much expression into them. Then I took off his cap and set it at a rakish angle and he reminded me that it was rude to listen to private conversations. I pushed the door open and walked in. Cousin David stood up and came to meet me, took my shoulders in his hands and looked down at me. He was awkward with me and I thought it likely that he had no experience of children. He pulled out a chair for me to sit down and then set Garry-monkey on a chair by himself, even straightened a cushion so that he could lean back comfortably. The sitting room was very big by my standards and it was furnished with chintz covered chairs, deep and comfortable.

There were two windows that looked out into darkness and there was such a silence as I had never felt, as if we had come to a land of complete isolation, where no people lived. The light was golden-mellow from a lovely old globe lamp, that had been converted to electricity. There was a similar lamp on the top of the desk unlit and here Hamish sat with his chin on his hands, not missing a move I made. We made conversation about my dress and about my bedroom and I said it was a Snow White's bedroom and thanked Cousin David for everything, tried to thank him, but he would not listen to my thanks. He stood up at last and stretched his arms towards the ceiling, said he must change back into the kilt, for he was in civilisation again and it was more fitting than the trews. He left Hamish and me alone and there was awkwardness between us, that went on and on. I sat in the centre of the chair and knew it was too big for me and that I was lost in it. Hamish fidgeted about the room, going to the book-case and opening it as if he was searching for something to read. I tried to think of some topic of conversation, but my head was empty. The silence stretched out between us and stretched out to the mountains and to the rivers and to the seas. I knew I must break it, for it was an unhappiness, that I could not understand. He had his back to me, did not turn round when I put the question to him, as it swam into the goldfish bowl of my brain.

"Is it true what Cousin David said, that he got you in a will too?"

He did not move, just stiffened and stood still as a statue, and I had to go on with it, having just started, for he made no answer.

"Are you a relative of his or are you an orphan too?"

He put the book back in the case and closed the glass doors and came over to the fire and fiddled with the tobacco bowl on the mantelshelf and now he watched me in the mirror.

"You could say he got me in a will, if you were given to talking in a fancy way," he said. "As to the other query, I'm an orphan and a relative and I've been here for six years."

He turned round with a swing of the kilt and now he looked down at me and there was kindness in his eyes and amusement too, for he nodded his head at Garry-monkey and asked me if yon animal was comfortable or was the chair as big for him as mine was for me.

I settled myself more squarely in my chair and told him I was quite at home and then thought of the meaning of what I said and felt pain in my chest again. He saw it too and came over to take a plait in his hand and smile at me, told me that we were a gey fine pair of folk, the Garry-monkey and myself. Then he was back at the fire, watching me in the mirror.

"My father died six years ago. We came here, my mother and I. Then she died. There was nowhere to go. David Sutherland was my closest relative and he made me welcome."

"But if you're his kin, you're mine too."

"I'm no blood kin to you," he told me shortly, as if he disowned me. "I'm related to him through my father. You're on his mother's side."

Maggie came in at that moment, with two dogs at her heels, told me she had kept them shut in the kitchen till I had settled in. They were black and white sheepdogs and they crept in apologetically, with their stomachs to the carpet, the whites of their eyes pleading against dismissal. Soon they were twining themselves in ecstasy against my ankles, resting their heads on my lap, snuffling with inquisitive noses against Garry-monkey. They were working dogs, Tammy and Bess, Hamish told me. They had no right to the sitting room, but they had the run of the house. If I did not watch out, they might both be in my bed when I woke up in the morning. I stroked their soft coats and they looked into my eyes and then turned to gaze at the plate of "Scots tablet", that Maggie had brought me. I had heard of that often enough and knew it was what I called 'fudge' and Maggie was warning me that I must not sample it before supper, or I might not do justice to the fowl. It was ready now and we were only waiting for Himself. He came in as she spoke in the kilt and the velvet jacket, the lace at his cuff, the dirk in his stocking. Did I not know well enough the glory of a Scots gentleman in the dress kilt? I was quite overcome by it now. He took my hand to bring me into the dining room across the hall and Tammy and Bess followed at our heels. I was to sit at the foot of the table. Maggie herself put me in my place and told me I was the new mistress of Old Jethart and the dogs were gracious enough to station themselves one on either side of me, as if they did me honour too. I looked at the snowy tablecloth, at the shining silver and glass, at Hamish on my left hand and at Cousin David at the table's head and remembered my mother's description of it. There should be a painting over the fireplace. I searched for it and found it, a lady in a white low-cut dress, with a swathe of

Sutherland tartan on her shoulder, her hair dressed in a fashion long past, her eyes watching me, her lips smiling. There was a story about her, but I did not know it. She had lived in Old Jethart a very long time ago and there had been unhappiness and tragedy. My mother had hinted at it, but never told me the details.

"It was all hundreds of years ago, honey. It's best forgot."

We had hare soup to start with and then "the fowl." I had not known such food to exist. The bread rolls were fresh baked and the potatoes were cooked, unpeeled, in the oven and served in table napkins in a silver ring. The trifle that followed was laced with sherry and thick with cream and my mind was back in the two-room tenement with Mother...

"The milk stands in earthenware vats for the cream to rise, against the churning. There's a tin cup with a curved handle, that you dip into it. You never tasted anything like it in all your born days, with the richness that's in it..."

I could hear her voice again, as clearly as if she stood by my side. I could feel her presence in the room, as if her spirit had taken flight and come home to Old Jethart, moving miraculously and silently and with the speed of thought, as maybe spirits do move. I put out a hand to grope the emptiness for her. For a moment, I was lonely and lost and desolate of spirit and then Hamish was laughing at me and telling me about Christmas. He spun my thoughts around and they went flashing past one stop after another, like the pin on a roulette wheel, slowing down, slowly and more slowly till the thought of Christmas blotted out all other thoughts.

"Unless it snows too hard in the night, we'll go up the hills tomorrow with Judy in the trap and fetch the Christmas tree."

I was quite engrossed in the magic of obtaining a Christmas tree by such a method. We had never aspired to one in the flat, but if we had, it would have been bought in the greengrocer's and carried home through the streets. It did not seem possible that a person could drive up a hill and cut a tree and carry it home in a pony trap. I wondered if Hamish was joking, but next day, I found he was not. We set out early after breakfast, protected against the weather with a hot bottle and a plaid rug. The roads were mere lanes, with grass that grew along the centre and the mountains were clad with Christmas trees, enough for the whole world. Maggie had packed us a picnic lunch and we ate it on the top of an iced hill, while Judy crunched her way through a truss of clover, thrown down for her by Hamish.

Then we were on our way home and he let me hold the reins, while we talked in a companionable way, mostly about school. He had been at a boarding school and he knew French and Latin and German. Cousin David would probably not let me go away to school. There had not been much time to make decisions, but Hamish thought it likely that I would go to the local school. It was closed for Christmas, but it would open again in the new year. I wouldn't get "the extras" there, just the plain reading, writing and arithmetic. Cousin David had asked Hamish if he would start me off on "the extras." If that plan were carried out, I might study in the evenings with Hamish. He grinned over at me, as Lady Judy took the trap down the road at a cautious trot.

"You'll have to watch out," he warned me, "I'm a terrible hard master, but don't worry your head about it till after Christmas. Don't spoil the season with thoughts of what's to come after Hogmanay. All the same, I hope you keep your copy books tidy..."

So we came back to Old Jethart and entered by the white gate and drove up the twists of the avenue and the river was far below and the house sentinel above.

It was a happy afternoon, as we put the tree in the hall. It had been bound with twine and laid along the trap. Now it was eased down and carried up the six steps and freed from its bondage. Then there was a round tub with stones to hold the tree firmly. Auld Rob came in from the stable and nailed struts of wood to hold it in place and Maggie had a box of lights that she had got all the way from Inverness. They blinked out and in and in and out and I hopped from one foot to the other, till Hamish warned me not to wear out the floor.

I was to have many Christmasses at Old Jethart and the first of them was the pattern of them all. I had come into a new world. Mother had not exaggerated when she had said it was "paradise". The week before Christmas, Cousin David took Maggie and me into Oban in the car, to do the shopping. Arrived there, he gave me what seemed a fortune to put in my purse, told me that it was to buy presents and that it was all very secret. I must go round the shops by myself. It was the strangest experience to go shopping in Oban. Up to then, my transactions in shops had been many. I was quite accustomed to take a carrier bag and walk round a supermart, picking out washing powders and matches and vinegar and boot polish and shop bread and salt, salt, salt. The money would be ready in my hand and I had to keep the sum in my head . . . not let the list grow too long, nor the price too high. There were things on offer to be snatched up, that might have shot skywards like the beanstalk by next week. There was a pushing of people and a brightness of light and hurry and scurry and bustle . . . a race to the "out" of the cash desks. In the street, the traffic roared by, slowed by the town, fuming, noisy, reverberating. It was no pleasant thing to go shopping. The day we went to Oban, I did not realise that "doing the messages" had a magic about it. Maybe I was apprehensive about being alone in a strange place. Cousin David had gone to see the solicitor. Maggie had settled herself down in the grocer's with a shopping list on the counter. I wandered along the street and turned down a little lane and so found myself back on the sea front. There was an Aladdin's Cave of a shop and the sound of the sea in my ears and a sharp wind and the shrilling of gulls and the smell of salt.

I went into Aladdin's Cave and stood astonished at so much wealth set out before me. All the money in the world could not buy such "emeralds and amethysts and gold moidores." This was a cargo such as Masefield had described. I half turned to go, but there was a lady at my side. She had time to listen to what I wanted. I confided to her how much I wished to spend, told her that I was worried about pleasing Auld Rob. Perhaps I spilled a little of my story to her. Otherwise, surely she could never have taken the trouble she did to help me? There were trays of brooches. We divided the money out carefully . . . set it on the counter to see how we could make it go the farthest. This brooch for Maggie and that for May . . . and the battle axe, which was of Iona marble for Auld Rob. He was to wear it in his muffler from that Christmas Day. I never recall seeing him without his pin in all the years I knew him. There was a shop nearby, kept by a friend of the lady in the Cave of Jewels. They both put their heads together and between us we picked two pairs of knee stockings and two woven ties to match for Cousin David and Hamish. Gentlemen like that would have enough jewellery by them and you might not know what would suit them. Now everything must be wrapped carefully and hidden away till Christmas morning . . . and when I came to town again. I must be sure to come and see them.

I stood at the rail on the sea front and looked out at the little ships that danced in the bay, looked over at the lonely house on the island and thought what a Robinson Crusoe place it was to live in. The sun was glinting on the water as if there were silver fish with silver fins swimming there.

If only Mother had not died. All my life, I had promised her that I would work hard and get rich. I would buy her a fur coat and an emerald ring. It would have been perfect that day, if I could have chosen a present for her. There was a great cluster of turquoise all rough from the rock, with the crystal stones glittering like the Arabian Nights. It was what I would have picked for her . . . the most beautiful thing I had ever seen . . . and now Cousin David found me looking out at the island of Kerrera with the dreams of what might have been in my eyes.

We went to the Gem shop together and looked in the window and I confided some of my thoughts to him and he stood and looked at the split rock of turquoise and neither of us said anything for a long silence. He was sad that I knew he grieved for my loss. I challenged him with it, but he refuted the idea. He and I had the same trouble, he told me. I had said I had been worried about finding anything suitable for Auld Rob. He was in the same quandary. He laughed as he said it and the weariness was gone in a second. I had thought of a tam-'o-shanter. He caught the idea from me and took me to choose one in a shop near the Harbour. The many-coloured woolly cap was to become as familiar a sight in Old Jethart as the river and the white gate and the six shallow steps to the front door, but first of all there was Christmas . . . and Mother had been right to teach me that this house was Shangri-La.

I woke up on Christmas morning and explored the contents of my stocking. There was a wonder about the gifts, even now that I had long known there was no such thing as Santa Claus. There was a diary and a needle-book and a pillar box savings bank and a tin of bulls' eyes and a flash light and last of all, but best, a new jumper and cap for Garry-monkey in yellow . . . "a skein of yellow that's like the sun playing on ripe wheat," past and gone.

We ate an enormous breakfast, as we did every morning come to that. I could not get used to plenty. We had Scot porridge and a pile of fresh-made baps, a block of farm butter, bacon and eggs, toast, marmalade. It was a leisurely meal on

Christmas morning with the opening of presents. I cannot begin to enumerate all the gifts I received, only describe one. Lady Judy was led up the front steps, brought right into the hall, where her hooves clicked against the flags. She was to be my very own and she had a pride of harness, caparisoned as she was, as if for a knight of old. There was a new saddle, bridle, rug ... a dark blue rug with my initials in gold. There was nothing for it, but put on my kit and go riding. Hamish and Cousin David set off up the hills, one on either side of me and the sun warm for December and the gulls screaming over our heads.

Then later that day, when the darkness had come down the revelry really started. I was to wear my crimson dress and Maggie did my hair for me, loose round my shoulders, with a crimson ribbon round my head. I sat at the foot of the table and wondered if I might be dreaming. Surely such food could never exist ... a turkey, a whole ham, roast potatoes and celery ... colcannon and this I knew, for Mother had made it often. The Christmas pudding blazed in brandy, blazed even when it came to my plate. There were crackers on the table and almonds and raisins, and great home-made sugar sweeties in cut-glass dishes, and stuffed dates and stuffed walnuts and a dozen other delights.

When we were done, we came to the toasts and there was a moment of sadness when Cousin David got to his feet with his glass raised.

"To absent friends," he said and looked down the table at me and I knew we drank to Mother, wished she were there to see him as he stood in the magnificence of Highland dress.

The last part raised our hearts again, for Auld Rob came in as official piper, his kilt swaying as he walked back and forth, the colours bright on the tartan plaid over his shoulder. He gave us the old tunes, that were almost a religion to me, ending up with "I love a lassie, a bonnie, bonnie lassie" and he was kind enough to say it was all about myself, though he was to be harsh enough to me in the months ahead. Mother had told me that there would be "hell to pay" if she brought in a horse sweating and indeed he was a demon in the stables, but to me that night he was kindness itself, as indeed they all were. It was unlike any Christmas I had ever dreamed about, heard about, read about. It was as if I had come to a black door and known that I must go through it to torment, and then when I had come through it, I found a land of content and great joy and happiness and love. I understood why Mother had wanted to get back to Old Jethart. If you had lived there, you could never be happy outside its boundaries and I got the feeling in my heart that night, which was to bind me to Old Jethart for ever and ever, so that life away from it is only a half-life for me now. I can never be happy again till I go in by the white gate and ride up by the avenue, that twists around the hill and come once again to run up the six shallow steps and into the sitting room, to stand before the blazing fire and to throw my arms about the Laird's neck and tell him that I have come home to him again.

When Christmas was over, we settled into the routine of the farm and I began my studies under Hamish almost at once. He was the same as any elder brother might have been to me and I think it was a good thing, for Cousin David spoilt me. Looking back now, I see that Cousin David could never bring himself to say no to me, whereas it seemed Hamish's pleasure to thwart me in any way he could. He had plenty of opportunity for it in my lesson hours. Every evening I would get out my books and prepare to drive him crazy with my stupidity.

If I close my eyes I can see the sitting room as it was that first evening, when Hamish launched me on the study of the dead languages. There was a turf fire in the grate glowing pleasantly and the wind was roaring in the chimney like a lion. The red chenille velvet cloth had been spread on the table and a bowl of Christmas roses occupied the centre of it. Hamish and I sat side by side with my books, which had arrived up from Glasgow the day before, ready in a little pile before us. Cousin David was sitting in his arm chair by the fire, pretending to read a book, but not turning over the pages. He always seemed to be there, when I did my lessons at the table and he never concentrated on his book, but always on my lesson and I imagine Hamish did not like this very much.

Hamish opened the Latin Primer and the new-book smell was very pleasant to my nostrils.

"You have to get this off by heart," Hamish told me, running his finger down the first declension of nouns. He read it down for me in his deep, soft voice.

"Mensa, mensa, mensam, mensae, mensae, mensa. It's the word for a table in each of its cases."

"It sounds like poetry," I remarked to Cousin David and he agreed with me.

The white cat had come into the room from the kitchen to pay me a visit. She came over to my chair and got on her hindlegs very softly and then she stretched out a paw to touch my hand.

"Do you want to learn Latin, Snowball?" I asked her. "It won't help you to catch mice, you know."

I turned to Hamish.

"What's the Latin for Snowball, Hamish?" I asked him and Cousin David laughed.

"I should think that's stumped you, laddie," he said.

Hamish got ruffled.

"You'd be better to keep your mind on your first declension," he said dourly. "You can learn about snowballs, when we come to them and I'll thank you to stop playing with the cat and mind your book. Read it over to me now."

"Mensa, a table, nominative," I read. "Mensa, O table, vocative, Mensam, a table accusative."

"Have you done about cases in school?" Hamish asked me and I looked sideways at Cousin David and asked "Suit cases?" just to make him smile.

Hamish was quite unaware that I was making a game of it all and that I deserved the cane for it, but he kept his temper and went on with patience.

"You know what a noun is, I suppose?"

I nodded my head and told him it was the name of a person, place or thing, and Cousin David nodded his head in approval and this made Hamish scowl.

"Well then!" he said. "Nouns have cases, depending on how you use them. If a noun is the subject of the sentence, that is the main noun in the sentence, it's in the nominative case. If I say "The table is in the room," you'd use 'mensa'. Have you got that?"

I nodded my head and he went on with the lesson.

"If I am talking to a person, place or thing, it's in the vocative case. If I say "Oh, Belinda! Thou art being very stupid." Belinda is in the vocative case. If I am talking to the table, for example, I would say "O, Mensa," again and that means "Oh, table!""

"I wish I had known that at school," I sighed, again to amuse Cousin David and catching his eye with no trouble at all. "I could have said "Oh, table, thou art very hard!" when I came to the twelve times multiplication."

Cousin David was twisting the signet ring round the little finger of his left hand. He was delighted by my joke, but to Hamish it was the last straw, that broke the camel's back, as Mother would have said.

"I think we'd be better to do our lessons in the dining room," he declared stiffly. "There are too many diversionary activities here. If you think I am trying to teach you Latin for my own amusement, you're wrong. David asked me to get the damned stuff into your stupid head and I'm doing it to oblige him. My work here is to see after the sheep and the cattle and keep the horses exercised. It's no part of a steward's task to drum Latin into a lassie's head and if I have any more of your nonsense, you can get your book-learning from Auld Rob in the stables and it would be a more fitting place for it too."

I saw that he was really put out, so I stood up and put my arm round his neck and told him that I was sorry.

"I deserve to be slapped for it, Hamish," I told him. "Mother would have slapped me, if I had joked about anything she had been trying to teach me so patiently. Don't you think you'd better to give me a box on the ear?"

I leaned up against his side and tried to coax him into forgiving me.

"Mensa, mensa, mensam, mensae, mensae, mensa," I whispered up against his white collar, for I had learned it quite well and he laughed then and told me I was an ass with big ears. Of course, in a day or two, I provoked him again and again and again, but Cousin David was just as much to blame in encouraging my pertness. I was getting spoilt by too much kindness and the loss of adversity and I was as naughty as any small girl of nine can be. Hamish contented himself for a while by producing a red pencil. He would draw it through large bits of my homework and say "No!" and "No!" again. "I've told you a dozen times that it's not done like that! The girl has a table. The table of the girl is not the table of the queen. The girl loves the table of the queen. You've put every noun in the nominative case. It's all wrong."

"But you're talking about the table all the time. It's the important thing."

"Of course, it's not, you daftie! Is your brain softened with all the still lemonade you drank for supper? I'd rather plough the ten acre field than try to drive anything into your skull."

"I thought it wasn't too bad for a beginner, Hamish," Cousin David put it mildly.

74

"It's silly anyway," I declared. "Who wants to know about the table of the queen? I'd rather do about snowballs."

Hamish stood up abruptly and took a penknife out of his pocket.

"I'm going to try a new method of education," he exclaimed, very dour in the face and with his brows drawn down. "I'm away to the haggard this minute and I'm going to cut myself a sally switch. I'm sick of playing with you, you big-eared donkey and I'm sick of Cousin David and you winking behind my back."

He went off through the door at a great rate, with his kilt swinging and I sat in terror till he returned, for I thought he was going to beat me and I knew I deserved it richly. My bottom tingled in anticipation, for as far as I could see, Cousin David was going to make no move to save me. He had even nodded his head in approval at Hamish's action.

"I'm afraid you've called the tune," he laughed. "Now you've got to pay the piper, and the dominie is really vexed with you this time."

In my naughtier moments, I had taken to calling Hamish "Dominie", to tease him and sometimes I translated it into "Oh, Master!" and I could see that the day of reckoning was upon me. He came back again, looking just as black as before, switching a sally rod in his hand and frowning in a manner which made my heart thump in my chest. I thought I should die with shame if he beat me there in front of my guardian. My face got red with the thought of it. He threw the switch out of his hand down on the table before my nose.

"Now we'll introduce the new order of education in Old Jethart," he declared. "And I'll thank you to remember that there are two mirrors in the room and if you feel like winking at your Cousin David, you'd best wait till the lesson is over. If you wink at him, behind my back, I'll see it just as handy as if you do it before my eyes, and I'll put my switch to good use on your trews, Mistress McLean, and you'll not sit comfortable for a week, for I've got a strong arm and a quick temper. I want no more smudged copy books and no stupid mistakes, no pert talk and no little jokes for David's benefit yonder and it will be the better for your backside if you recall it in future."

Cousin David's eyebrows went up and I thought for a moment that he would take the switch from the table and put it in the fire, but instead of that, he laughed across at Hamish and quoted a piece of Shakespeare.

" 'A Daniel come to judgement! Yea a Daniel!

O wise young judge, how I do honour thee!' "

He came over to the table and stooped to kiss the top of my head.

"There's more learning got by the tawse than was ever got by kindness, lassie. I see Hamish has taken off the snaffle tonight and he's going to ride you in the curb bit, and I think he's a wise judge of his lassie, for she's spirited and wants careful schooling."

He went off out of the room then with a backward glance at Hamish.

"I'd not have you break her spirit, Hamish laddie," he said gently. "She has had enough to do it in this world already and I'd not like it done now."

"Don't bother yourself about the sally rod, sir," Hamish laughed. "It's a show of strength. That's all."

I did not understand what they were talking about. I did not know what a tawse was, but I soon found out in the school at Innish within the next few days.

PART THREE

The school was beside the Station and it was three miles from Old Jethart. It was a very strange place compared with the Junior School I had attended in England, which was a most modern up-to-the-minute place. I was used to great glass-sided class rooms and specially coloured blackboards and chalk, to prevent eyestrain. I was used to the science block, the library, the school band, the school choir, the changing rooms with showers, the neat rows of lockers, where one kept one's shoes and one's own hand-towel, marked with one's name. I was accustomed to very lady-like teachers, who talked with a plum in their mouths and were very genteel and polite. In my last year, we had even had a swimming bath, with water, which stung our eyes and smelt unpleasantly, because it had been made free of germs.

The school at Innish was a shock to my ideas of what a school should be. The snow was beginning to fall on the first day, when I went along with Cousin David to be introduced to the Schoolmaster. I rode Lady Judy and I was well used to her by then. I was to stable her at the Station-master's house every day and ride her home by myself in the evening. There were one or two other children who arrived on horseback, for it was a very lonely wild district and buses were few and far between.

The school consisted of one big room with bare scrubbed boards. There was a blackboard on an easel and a raised dais for the Master. The desks were in rows ranged down along in lines and each one held two pupils. There was an inkwell for each of them and a roomy compartment under the lid to keep books. The walls were hung with a series of maps and were lined with a wooden wainscot for the lower three feet. Apart from the school room, there was a boot room, where you hung your coat and there was a pump in the yard, with a stone trough under it, which supplied all the water we were likely to need. There were two very old earth closets at a distance of fifty yards from the school building, one marked Girls and the other Boys, but these were better avoided, as they were not very pleasant places.

The Dominie was a middle-aged man called "Johnny McGill" by all his pupils. He was a short, broad-chested man, with iron grey hair and the rubbery big-nose of the Scot. He ruled the school with the help of a strip of leather with a fringed end, and this, I soon learnt was called a "tawse". With the help of Mr. McGill and the tawse, I picked up more knowledge in one short year than I had been taught with gentle measures over the time I had spent in my old school. On that first day, he shook me by the hand, and told me that I was very welcome to Argyll and he hoped that he would be able to teach me something. I stood at his desk on the platform and felt sixty strange eyes looking at me with interest. It might have been a thousand and sixty, from the effect they had on me. They were aged from five to fifteen, I knew, and were all children from the surrounding crofts and farms in the mountains.

"I'll put you by Jeannie Stewart," said Johnny McGill, picking out a big girl, with long fair plaits to her waist. "Your mother's name was Mary Stuart and that's near enough for friendship. She'll look after you and see you don't come to harm and she's a mitherless bairn too, so perhaps she'll have a fellow-feeling for you . . . alone and in a strange country. 'A fellow feeling makes us wondrous kind,' as David Garrick said, so perhaps we'll see if he was right. Do you feel wondrous kind, Jeannie?"

Jeannie Stewart smiled at him and said she'd "dae her best wi' me" and I let go Cousin David's hand to which I had been clinging in a babyish way and sat down in the desk beside her.

Mr. McGill went to see Cousin David off the premises and the most awful noise broke out at once in the class room. I had never heard anything like it in my other school. There were two boys down in the corner fighting like wild animals and a ring of other boys around them, shouting at the tops of their voices. Four of the girls were up at the blackboard drawing a portrait of Mr. McGill to the approval of the rest of the class.

"What's your name?" whispered Jeannie in my ear. "Is it true you're awa' frae London? How lang will ye bide at the big hoose? Are you kin to the Laird then? Is he your uncle?"

I was very nervous of the whole place. I smiled at her and told her that Mother had died before Christmas and the Laird was her first cousin. He had been kind enough to give me a home and I would stay there for ever, as far as I knew.

"Did your father not think o' wedding another?" she asked me. "My pappy wed a second wife and she skelps me terrible hard, if I do the slightest thing. My hairt is broken wi' her."

I told her that Father was dead too and she said it was better like that, than to have a step-mamma, who skelpit you twice a day for naething at all.

She asked me if I liked the school and I said that I did not know yet.

"Ye'll like it weel," she said. "Dinna greet when we go oot in the yard and the boys duck you. It's done to new bairns, to put a name on them, but it only means that they hold you under the pump a wee while. It'll nae do ye any harm."

My heart was full of fear and foreboding with this dreadful prospect, but I tried to put a brave face on it. Johnnie McGill came back into the room and the Pastor was with him and we started off the day with the scripture lesson. The Pastor singled me out for great attention, as I was the only new child. He came walking down to my desk and asked me if I knew the ten commandments, and I could not even think of one of them in my fright. He was a tall thin man with a cross manner and he seemed over-fond of the use of the dreadful thing they called a tawse. He stood by my desk beating time to his words with the leather strap on the wooden surface.

"I dinna think that they pay much attention to God's holy word away in England," he said. "They're all too inter-es-ted in the worrld, the flesh, and the devil doon there, to teach children the catechism. It's aye a pursuit of pleasure and gold ... the worship of the golden calf, that is happening today all ower again, like in the days o' the prophet Moses."

I was "ducked" at lunchtime and it was a dreadful ordeal, as I had known it would be. We had not been released to the yard five minutes, when the bigger boys made a ring around me and started to chant:

"What's your name? What's your name? What's your name?"

Jeannie tried to hunt them away, but the boys cared nothing for any girl, no matter how big. The male was supreme in Innish School, as Hamish told me later.

The other children crowded round us to see the fun and the boys went on with their horrible chant.

"Belinda," I answered in a small voice.

"But the Minister baptised ye in England?" cried the biggest boy, whom I recognised as being the ring-leader. "Have you no' been received into the true Church o' Scotland?"

"That's blasphemy, Jock McGregor!" Jeannie cried from the back of the crowd, but her voice fell on deaf ears.

Jock McGregor was a red-headed lanky boy, with red childblains on his fingers and the knees out of his trews. I had plenty of experience in dealing with such as he, in the town school and my knowledge stood me in good stead. I knew it was useless to try to fight the lot of them, so I went along to the pump very quietly, with two boys gripping my arms.

"What name will we gie her?" shouted Jock McGregor and I stood there red in the face with shame, while suggestions poured in from every side. It was a very cold day, with the snow coming down in drifting flakes out of a grey sky. The breath clouded from our mouths in the frosty air. I tried to smile, but I did not succeed very well with it.

"We'll call her 'Corbie,'" said my red-headed enemy at last. "She's as black in the heid as an auld black corbie."

He caught me by the nape of the neck and thrust my head under the spout of the pump, and a dozen willing hands supplied the power to raise the water. I felt it gush out all over the back of my head and the top of my yellow sweater, drenching my long hair. I hoped it would be dry before I got home, or Maggie might scold. I tore myself away from my chief tormentor, but faced him still, knowing that he wasn't done with me yet.

He stuck his hands into his pockets and looked at me coolly.

"My ma says that she's the lassie of a drunken sot," he jeered at me. "He was a Captain in the Highland Regiment, but they thrown him oot. He was a dirty drunken bastard."

"That's a lie," I said and clenched my fists. "That's a dirty lie and I'd thank you to take it back."

"I'll no' tae it back," he shouted. "Because it's God's truth. You ask anybody, that knew Captain McLean. He was aye as drunk as a fiddler's bitch."

I saw that Hamish had appeared from somewhere and was coming across the yard slowly, but I had been trained in a hard school and I knew how to fight my own battles.

"Say that again," I challenged Jock McGregor.

"Your feyther was a drunken bastard," he obliged.

My clenched left fist took him straight up the nostrils and I got a savage delight in seeing the blood spurt in two thick streams down his upper lip. A dark scrawny looking boy, who was his special friend jumped at me like a shabby leopard, but I saw him coming. I stepped to one side, like any boxer and I dealt him an open-handed blow across the face with my right hand and for good measure gave him a back-hander across the other side of his face, for I saw he was not finished by the first one. The second crack hurt my knuckles and brought him up short and the ring of boys widened around me. Master McGregor was wiping the blood from his mouth with his red, chilblained hand and I suddenly felt sorry for what I had done, for suddenly he looked beaten and hungry and poor. I took out my handkerchief and went over to him, smiled at him although my lips were stiff with fright. I wiped the blood off his mouth and chin gently and I told him that I was sorry for hurting him.

"My!" he exclaimed with a grin of admiration. "My! You're a bonnie fichter and no mistake."

I saw that the victory was mine. I clenched my fists again and I looked round at them.

"My father was a brave man and a good soldier. He served his country and his king," I said. "If any of you want to say anything else about him, say it now, but if it's a lie, like Jock's was, I'll push it back down your throats. My father is dead and he can't speak up for himself, but I can speak up for him, so if there's anything to be said, say it now ..."

Jock McGregor put his arm around my shoulders.

"I'll take back what I said," he laughed. "He mun ha' been a brave bonnie fichter to have sich a lassie."

He gave me a comradely hug, and went on "I'm your mon from this day forth, Corbie McLean. If you want any battles fichting for you, just gie a wee whistle on your fingers for Jock McGregor and he'll come tae to your side."

We did not get any further with the affair that day, for

Johnnie McGill came out to the playground with a dour face on him and he was swinging his tawse in his hand. I got a feeling of fear in the pit of my stomach, for I saw that it was time to unite against a common enemy, who, I knew well, could not be put to flight by a punch on the nose.

I was riding back from school that afternoon on Lady Judy, who was in a hurry to get home through the snow to her warm stable, when Hamish stepped out from a gap in the hedge about a mile from Old Jethart. He fell in beside me and walked along very companionably, but in his silent way, he said nothing.

"Thank you for coming to my help this morning," I said after a while.

He had his gun under his arm and he turned round to look up at me.

"I didn't think you saw me," he said.

"I saw you all right," I told him. "And it was very kind of you."

"Och! You didn't need any help," he laughed. "I know that school well and I thought that they'd try your mettle this morning and I also thought that it might be a shock for a poor wee black mousie, on the first day at her new school in the Highlands. I found out that you're not such a prim little miss, as you look, and I found out that, with all your bad behaviour in my own private tuition, you can behave yourself right gallantly in the face of overwhelming odds."

I took this as a great compliment from him, but I did not say anything and after a while, he went on.

"Yon left was a beautiful blow . . . couldn't have bettered it myself. I went off after you hit the other fellow the backhander, across the snout. It's best if a lassie can fight her own wars. You'll do fine now. Jock McGregor is your man for life and he's head of the whole of Innish."

We went on for a quarter of a mile, both feeling very

friendly towards each other. Then he spoke again.

"How did you get on with McGill? Did he give you a taste of the tawse?"

I hung my head at that, for indeed, I had not got on very well with the dominie.

"I got two strokes on the hand, when we came in out of the yard. He saw the state my hair was in and he was wild with me. Poor Jock McGregor got six across the seat of his trews. It rose the dust out of him. He told me after that it made him forget the pain in his nose, but he was just being brave about it all."

Hamish caught the pony by the head and pulled us to a halt.

"And what did McGill give you the tawse for?" he demanded indignantly. "He must have known that you didn't wet your own hair."

I glanced down at him diffidently.

"Actually, it was because I wouldn't tell who did."

I had found that standards were different in Innish. One told. I had made quite a heroine of myself in the school, simply by holding my tongue. Johnnie McGill chose to think that I was being stubborn and challenging his authority, and that if he let me get away with it, the whole school would follow my example. I had stood quite miserably by his desk, while he swung the tawse in his hand, asking me, for the last time, to tell him who poured water over my hair.

"Very weel then. Hold your hand out."

I put out my hand very gingerly and his went up to his shoulder, with the tawse waiting to descend on my shaking palm. Jeannie Stewart and Jock McGregor jumped to their feet at that very minute. Jeannie named the chief culprits, but poor Jock said that he did it. His red sore hands were shaking with terror. I pulled back my hand with a sigh of relief, for I had been saved at the last moment.

"You can stretch out your hand again, Mistress McLean.

You're not out o' the wood yet. The fact that McGregor has confessed his sin doesn't blot oot the fact that you stood there and defied my authority. You refused to obey my commands. What sort o' a school would it be, if ye all started to behave in yon outlandish fashion? Ye can keep your Sassenach ideas to yoursel', Mistress. I'll thank you to remember not to let them loose here, and when I ask ye a question, it's to be answered, or ye'll maybe get what I'm going to gie McGregor now."

Hamish seemed to approve of my action in not telling.

"So you martyred yourself for the common weal?" he said looking up into my face. "Let's see your hands."

I took off my yellow string gloves and he bent his dark head over my palms and ran a gentle finger over the red marks.

"McGill has a bonnie stroke," he remarked and then looked up at me keenly and shot out "What did yon boy say in the playground, that made you stand up to him like that?"

I pulled on my gloves and clicked my tongue at Lady Judy and she walked on impatiently towards her stable. She disapproved of all this delay on the road home. I made no answer to Hamish and he prompted me again.

"It might be a thing I could help with and it might not," he said.

I could feel the red colour flowing up over my face, and I still said nothing, but held my head down and Lady Judy pulled at the bit to get trotting off down the road to the gate.

"Come on," said Hamish.

"He said that my father was a bad man," I got out at last.

"How was he supposed to be a bad man?"

His voice was dour and grim.

"Oh, Hamish! Must I tell you?" I asked him.

"Aye."

"He said that Father drank too much and that he was put out of the regiment."

"It's lucky for him I didn't hear him then or he'd have got

worse," said Hamish, opening the white gate for me.

I rode Lady Judy through and he shut it again after us, and my pony went to the side of the drive to crop the long grass, nuzzling her nose into the thin coating of snow, as if she were starving.

"Did you know Father?" I asked him.

He made no attempt to go on up the avenue. Instead, he climbed up on the gate and sat perched on top of it and took out his pipe and started to fill it, just like as if it were midsummer, and his bare knees not red with the cold.

"I met him once or twice," he said looking across at me, with his eyes very dark.

"There's more snow on the way," he said then and looked up at the sky and sighed.

"Cousin David told me that Father was a brave man," I volunteered. "He said that he was a brave soldier and that I was to be proud of him."

He still said nothing and I wondered why he had perched himself up on the gate, and had started to fill his pipe, as if the sun was shining and the birds were singing and it was a good day to laze about.

"If you don't hear it from me, you'll hear it from another," he murmured almost to himself. "And you might get the wrong idea."

He stopped there and he said nothing more for a good three minutes. He pretended that he could not get his pipe going and he got down and searched round for a small twig to push through the stem of it, but he could not find one to his taste and so he climbed back up on the gate and filled the pipe from his tobacco pouch and lit it and it went very well, even without being cleaned out with the twig.

"Your father was a fine man," he said at last. "He was as braw a fighter as you are yourself. There was nothing he was afraid of . . . nothing."

"But what might I hear from someone else then?" I enquired curiously.

"He had one great weakness," he told me looking down at the pipe in his hand, as if he had never seen it before and wanted to study it in every detail.

"He was aye a man to drink," he went on. "Even before he met your mother, he had a taste for it. It got the better of him in the finish, for it was the one enemy that he couldn't fight. People thought that when he wed your mother he'd give it up. He did too, for a couple of years, but then he was at it again, for you can't teach an old dog new tricks. It was bad for her too, for she must have seen your grandfather . . . och! don't bother about that for now."

I said nothing. I sat on Lady Judy's back and knew why Mother had always talked about Old Jethart and never about Father.

"Did you not wonder why your mother had no pension?" he shot out at me, and then answered his own question with "No! I suppose you'd not know what a pension was."

I knew that Mr. Higgins had a thing called a pension from the war, because he had got a piece of shrapnel in his leg and walked lame. I knew it was money that the country paid to a soldier. Now I saw suddenly that Mother and I should have had money like that too, if something terrible hadn't happened. I knew that there was some black thing that I did not know.

"I'll take it very kindly, Hamish, if you could tell me what happened," I said quietly. "Then I'll know what I can say, if people hint things at me, or even shout them out at me, like Jock McGregor did today."

"He was cashiered from the Army, Lindy. Do you know what that means?"

"It means that Jock was right. They threw him out. Perhaps I shouldn't have hit Jock after all. Eh?"

"You should have hit him all right," he said grimly. "It was not a gentlemanly thing to shout into a lady's face and I think you taught him different too. Your father did nothing scandalous. He just could not leave the bottle alone, like many a fine man before him. He drove a car, when he had no right to drive it and he was caught at it and he did it again and again. He had no luck. He was sent to prison for it and the Army was done with him then."

I began to walk the black pony slowly up the avenue and a great deal of little things, that I did not understand, clicked into their proper answers in my mind. Hamish was walking by my side with his hand on my knee.

"It broke your mother's heart, for she could do nothing with him and she hid herself from friends, who could have helped her. Cousin David scoured the whole country after her. He let the whole farm go to pot, while he did it too. Then in one year, you were born and your father died and she was very ill and there was no way of finding her. The news came a roundabout way. Cousin David never found her . . . never knew where she was . . . till your letter came on the Monday morning, as we sat down to lunch. He was going to take the evening train . . . had his bag packed, when the phone rang and there was the English doctor on it, to tell him she was gone."

My heart was like a lump of lead in my chest. The snow was beginning to fall again, in great lazy flakes, that floated silently down.

"It was an illness with him," Hamish was saying. "He was not to blame for it, any more than if he had been born with a crooked back. He served his country well. He was a brave soldier and a fine man. You're to be proud of him, the way every lassie must be proud of her father."

I looked down at the reins in my yellow gloved hand and wondered if it had been Father's fault. He could have fought against it. Surely he could have fought anything for Mother's sake? He must have known he was breaking Mother's heart. She would never have broken his. There was something else I did not know. There was a mystery that I had not solved, but in time, I would know it all. Father had not drunk to excess for two whole years after his marriage. Hamish had just told me that. I asked myself if something had happened to overcome him, something that made him seek the comfort of a dram and another and another. Why had Mother talked always about Cousin David and never about him? Why had she left her heart in Old Jethart, for it seemed to me that she had done just that. The pony's hooves were beating a tune in my ears, as she walked on the thin carpet of snow. I put a hand down to clutch Hamish's hand, which rested on my knee. The burn from Johnny McGill's tawse hardly filtered through the black thoughts in my brain.

"The Garry-monkey has black thoughts, Hamish. They're mine really but I put them into his mouth. If I were to tell him what you just told me, he'd say that there was more to it . . . that you hadn't told me the whole of the story. There's a mystery about Old Jethart and it's to do with people who were there and are there no more, just as it's to do with Cousin David and with you and with me . . . There are secrets you're not telling me . . ."

"Yon creature is as canny as a bag of foxes then," he laughed, and stretched up his arms to lift me to the ground, for we had come to the foot of the six steps. He turned to look up at the polished windows and the wink of the brass knocker against the white front door.

"The whole place is full of mystery, not just today but in time long past. There's a lady who walks in the full of the moon and sings a wee song. There's a troop of horses, that comes galloping down the drive to the steps there. There's a horseman that sits on a steed of black . . . a steed with jewels on his head, no less . . . God have mercy on us! There's a curse on the place, that'll be lifted one day . . . and black is white and white is black . . . and hearts are broken in dozens or one by one. It's all a pack of nonsense and don't believe a word Maggie says about it, nor yet May . . . least of all Auld Rob. When he starts off on it, block up your ears against him, or you'll find yourself as daft as he is."

Auld Rob came round from the stables at that moment and looked at me dourly.

"Ye'll never be the fine jock yer mither was," he said. "Ye dinna put your mind tae it. Ye sit up there like ye might sit on a bean pole and the pony tak's ye where she's got a mind tae go. Ye wait for Mister Hamish to lift ye doon. I daresay ye let the beast graze doon by the gate, for she's got grass in her mooth the noo."

I was surprised at the way Hamish came to my defence, for he turned on Auld Rob, with no reason in the world, or so I thought.

"Hold your tongue, you old daftie," he cried. "The lassie held the whole school at bay today. She bled McGregor's nose for him and she near stretched Dermot Ruadh on the broad of his back, with two welts on the gob. Then she took the blame on herself and had the tawse the first day, with no sin on her soul. McGill is an old fool and you're another. I'll thank you to remember that she's been riding that mare for two-three weeks. Her mother was born in the saddle . . . brought up in it too. No thanks to her, if she can stop a mount snatching a wee mouthful of grass . . . lep' a five barred gate, break in horses . . . break men's hearts . . . Oh, Lord! You're a fool, Rob, and if I hear any more like yon out of you, I'll put my foot up your backside for you."

Auld Rob was astonished, as well he might be.

"Losh, Mister Hamish! Wha's got into ye, the day? I said nothin' tae upset ye."

Hamish wheeled on his heel and took me up the steps at

speed, stooped down when we got to the top and kissed my cold cheek.

"Don't let anybody tell you that your father wasn't a brave man. He was a braw bonnie fighter. He could beat every enemy in the world except one . . . the last one of all. It was no shame to him."

We found Cousin David at his desk in the sitting room, and I put my arm round his neck and told him I was home again. That was to be the formula of all my home-comings from that day on. I told him the sunny-funny things, about the Minister and his opinions of the Sassenachs, about how Johnny McGill was going to drive a good education into me with the aid of the tawse, if the tawse did not wear out before I did. So life settled down into a certain pattern and I was happy and content.

Hamish and the Dominie drove a great amount of knowledge into my head over the next few years. I never had the sally switch from Hamish, though Johnny McGill gave me my fair share of the tawse at Innish School. There was a toughness about Hamish all the same. He treated me with rough justice, as an older brother might have done. He threw me into the river on the coldest day of Summer, if we went swimming and I hesitated on the bank. He taught me to dive and then set me on the highest rock, marooned me there, till I jumped into the deep pool below. If I leapt in feet first, he took me to the height again and dared me not take a proper header. If Judy refused a jump, I must put her at it again and again. If I fell off her back, he put me up again and faced me back at the fence. He showed no interest in my bruises, less in my tears. If I scamped my worked in the stables and Auld Rob reported me, he took me there by the ear and made me do the task again, but properly. There was no kindness or gentleness in him, or so I thought, but I was wrong, as I was wrong about so many things. Over the next few years, I did not manage to explain the mystery that had intrigued me. I spoke to Maggie and to May. Auld Rob was a mine of information, but he got his generations mixed. It was from him that I learned about my grandfather, Mother's father. He had been a rich landowner and he had lost his money. There was a picture called "The Scarlet Pimpernel" on, in Innish village hall the week Auld Rob told me about that. Between his version and my imagination, I pictured my grandfather in long white breeches, satin coat, and a highwayman's hat, a quizzing glass in his hand, gaming at the tables. I could not work out how a gentleman could lose money except by gambling, but of course, I painted the picture in colours far too vivid and got my dates wrong. "The lassies had tae find work," and "Mistress Constance cam' here to see to the hoose for Mister David." I knew Aunt Con had been house-keeper, but I had not realised it was of necessity. One night, when Maggie came to say goodnight to me, I sat up in bed with a plait down each of my shoulders and with my feet wrapped warm in my long Viyella nightdress and turned the conversation back to the past. May came in to bring me a glass of hot milk and she looked at me in amazement, as I gave her my version of my grandfather's misfortunes.

"Och, hinny, ye've been reading ower mony books for yer ain guid. Yer grandfather wasn't gaming at the tables like Beau Nash, whoever he might be. He lost his siller the way mony a mon does..."

Maggie broke in upon her at that and sent a warning look like a shot across her bows.

"Take care of the pennies and the pounds will take care of themselves. It was a big estate and it had a bonnie name. It was 'Cool-na-Grena'... 'a corner in the sun.' It's easy to lose money, wi' cattle. They had a well-stocked place, but no luck in the world... and your grandpa... your grandpa... he wasna weel... not weel in himsel'!"

I wondered if he had been mad. There was something they

were ashamed to tell me, so I changed to another facet of the mystery.

"And Aunt Con came over to Scotland to earn her living?"

Maggie was busy pulling back the curtains to open the window and let in the cold night air and I snuggled down among the pillows, and pulled the blankets up to my nose. She looked over her shoulder at me.

"What a thing to say!" she exclaimed. "Your Aunt Con came here to help oot. The Master was dead and Mister David was alane. He wanted a body to take charge o' the hoose."

"Then Mother came here for two weeks and stayed six months."

"Aye, she did."

"Maybe if the family had been ruined and they had all to go out to work, maybe they sent her over here to see if she could find a rich husband?" I threw out, and Maggie and May poured scorn on my head. They knew all my reading of books and all the speaking of foreign tongues would turn my brain, but they did not expect it to have turned already. I was as bad as Auld Rob and if I did not walk cannily, I might find myself walking up the steps of the lunatic asylum, and they knew I was havering on just so as they would not turn off the light and tell me to go to sleep . . . and what was more, if they found me reading under the bedclothes with the wee pencil torch burning, they would tell Cousin David about it and I would find myself getting skelpit . . .

So I lay in bed in the darkness and worked it out. My grandfather had lost Cool-na-Grena some way and the fortunes of the family had taken a turn for the worst. One day, I might retrieve them. One day I might fall in love . . . and indeed I did, the Christmas I was thirteen years and a bit old, but I did not fall in love with a rich man, for I fell in love with Hamish, who was as poor as myself. The years had gone by. I was turned thirteen and Christmas was upon us again, when it happened. The Minister and his wife had been asked to supper on Christmas Eve and they brought with them a niece of theirs, a fair-headed plump girl, who was staying on a visit. I remembered the description of Hamish's ideal woman. Had I not overheard it, not two hours after my arrival at Old Jethart years before, as I reached the foot of the stairs?

"I don't like dark lassies . . . too much of the crow about them. I'll find a fair-haired lass, with eyes like the sea . . . and a sweet way to her . . ."

After supper, we played all the old games. Maggie and May joined in and we had *consequences* and *pass the parcel* and *I spy with my little eye* and *animal, vegetable or mineral* and *happy families* and *dumcrambo*. Then Maggie took the Minister and his wife off to look at a new stove in the kitchen and there was a lull in activities. Hamish took the fair girl by the hand and led her to the centre of the room, gave her a lingering kiss under the mistletoe . . . and my world was in ruins. I could not think why I should care whom he kissed, or why or where. Like St. Paul on the road to Damascus, I had a tremendous revelation. I loved Hamish with all my heart. I wanted more than anything to stick a dagger between the Minister's niece's ribs. I loved Hamish and I would love him till the day I died. I did not know how long I had loved him and not known it, but I knew it now without any doubt whatever.

People should not laugh at the suffering of jealousy, especially when the sufferer is thirteen years of age, with legs grown to a coltish length and with small, shameful thrusting breasts, twin peaks of shyness. I got a shaft of pain, when his lips came down on hers, a pain as sharp as death. I cannot even recall her name now, or where she lived when she was at home, or what became of her. He had chosen her as his partner all the evening, had sat by her side at supper, had picked her as the target of his jokes. I had set his place on the other side of the table and he had deliberately moved it across to her side.

I had glowered at them both from my place as Mistress of Old Jethart at the foot of the table.

I think Cousin David saw what was going on. He made much of me and singled me out for praise and attention, but his admiration was spurious coin. It went on all the evening. Hamish even kissed the girl goodnight, when the Minister's back was turned, on the top of the six shallow steps. Then he went off down the drive with them in their car to open the gates for them and I knew it was just because he wanted to prolong his time with her.

I turned back into the house with Cousin David and he laughed at my rueful face and said that it was his considered opinion that Hamish had had too much "Old Mull" on his plum pudding.

"I don't know what he saw in her," he smiled. "She's like a bonnie wee pig wi' a dress on."

I sat in my usual place by the fire and remembered how small I had been when I first sat there. Cousin David took one of my plaits in his hand and there was a melancholy mood stealing over him.

"One of these days, you'll ask my permission to put your hair up on your head. Maybe that's not the done thing now, but I daresay the hair will go up into a bee-hive with or without my say so. You'll marry and go away from me and this will be a lonely place again."

I sat looking into the fire as if I could read the future in the soft glow of the peat. I was quite sure that I knew how it would be, but I fell short of knowing what fate can do.

"I'll never go away," I said in a low earnest voice. "I'm the Mistress of Old Jethart and that's what I want to be to the day of my death. When a person comes here, there's a kind of magic . . . It's the beauty and the warmth and the kindness and the feeling of being welcome and wanted. My mother knew it too. Old Jethart put a spell on her and it put a spell on me. There's no happiness away from it for me, any more than there was for her."

I had added to his melancholy and I was sorry for it, said I would never be able to repay his kindness to me. I made a joke of it, told him that he could ask for anything up to half the value of my kingdom. He laughed at that, but there was no joy in his laughter, only a deep seriousness.

"There is something you have that I'd like . . . You could have it back . . ."

I could not understand the deep undercurrent to our conversation. Half an hour before, we had been playing happy families and the room had been full of laughter. Now the ghost of Mary Stuart had come to stand at the fire 'twixt him and me.

"There's a wee book of poetry you have . . . bound in white leather. I'd like to have it for my lifetime . . ."

I was out of the room in the flash of a smile, back again in a tumbling race down the stairs and a jump into the hall. The book was in his hand and he was turning open the fly leaf.

"It's good of you to let me have this. I'll seee you get it back . . ."

He was smiling now, but there was a look in his eyes that broke my heart.

"I'll make sure you get it back . . . put a codicil in my will about it."

He opened the book at the place it was always opened, this book of poems by Elizabeth Barrett Browning. His eyes were going down the lines I knew by heart . . .

>How do I love thee? Let me count the ways.
>I love thee to the depth and breadth and height
>My soul can reach, when feeling out of sight
>For the ends of beauty and ideal grace.
>I love thee to the level of every day's

Most quiet need, by sun or candle light.
I love thee freely as men strive for right.
I love thee purely as they turn from praise . . .
I love thee with the breath,
Smiles, tears of all my life! And if God choose,
I shall but love thee better after death . . .

He sat there looking down at it with the lines deep on his face in the shadow on the brass globe lamp. I remembered the inscription in the front of the book. I had but to close my eyes to see it, written plain in his own handwriting. I knew his writing by now, but it was not till this moment I recognised that the writing in the white book was his. "To Mary Stuart," he had written. "Whom I shall love till a' the seas gang dry . . . and the rocks melt wi' the sun . . ."

Of course, he had loved her. It explained everything . . . why he had been so sorrowful the first day he met me, why his hand had run up the banister rail to follow hers, the banisters in the tenement house, why he had said a hundred and one things that he had said. Of course, he had loved her . . . had hoped to marry her. As for her part, why had she got caught up in the web of Old Jethart, so that it was an ivory tower for her . . . a dream from which she might never awake? Had she loved him too? The floor opened like a pit at my feet as the thought came into my head. If she had loved him too . . . if she had run away with my father in a moment of infatuation, if she had come to realise that she had made an error of judging between one man and the next . . . Oh, God! It would explain so many things. It was the answer to the question of why my father had taken to drinking again. It was the answer why she had put in my head the dream of Old Jethart. It was the Garden of Eden, out of which she had cast herself. Her pride would stand at the gate with a sword, that turned every way . . .

I stood up and opened my mouth to ask him, but Hamish

came in and Cousin David was teasing him about his courtship of the Minister's niece. Hamish stood with his back to the fire and laughed. His words had no more importance to me than if he had been saying it was a fine night, for I had discovered that there are things that seem important, which have no real importance whatever.

"You didn't think I care a bawbee for yon fat piggeen?" he was saying in a most unchivalrous manner. "I only did it to spite the Minister. He didn't take his eyes off me the whole night, in case I got up to any of these disgusting modern carryings-on. I did it to send him up, for I can't abide his long thin nose. She's probably telling him all about it on the way home . . . and him preaching damnation and hell fire."

He came over to me and grabbed me by the hand, pulled me up to stand beside him.

"You're my lassie. Belinda! I'd give a cartload of the girl's fat favours, for a glance from your bonnie green eyes."

He kissed me under the mistletoe and he might have been charged with electricity for the effect his kiss had on me.

I was a child to him and he was treating me as if I were five years of age. He spun me round and gave me a sharp slap on the backside.

"Away off to your chair and sit still and behave yourself. It's in my mind to take you down to the Manse and tell the Minister you've been kissing a laddie under the mistletoe and you not turned fourteen yet. I don't know what the world is coming to."

He stretched his arms towards the ceiling and yawned . . . looked at me, where I sat in my chair, with my feet tucked under me.

"Till a' the seas gang dry, my lass, and the rocks melt wi' the sun. That's Robbie Burns' way and that's my way too, Mistress McLean . . . 'till a' the seas gang dry . . .'"

He could not have known what was written in the fly-leaf

of the white book of poems. It was just a co-incidence that he used that particular quotation, but Cousin David looked over at me and there was a silence, as if an angel passed overhead . . . and unsaid thoughts, that passed between him and me. Of course, he had loved her, but he did not know that I had recognised the writing . . .

Then Christmas went on as usual with all the fun of the season. That night, I woke and heard the song again. Maybe I dreamt that my mother came back to me. I had no recollection of dreaming. I woke up as the clock in the hall struck twelve of Christmas night and heard a small light voice, heard the familiar rhyme . . .

> "I had a little nut tree, nothing would it bear,
> But a silver nutmeg and a golden pear.
> The king of Spain's daughter came to visit me,
> And all for the sake of my little nut tree . . ."

I had not dreamt it. There was somebody in the room, singing in a high sweet voice. Had I not heard it often enough, awake and dreaming? My heart pounded in my chest and I felt bewitched.

"Mother?" I whispered and again "Mother?" I sat up in bed and stretched out my hands to her, but there was nobody there. In the bright of the moon, I could see the door closing, as if a draught moved it and the voice got fainter. I got up and went to the door, looked along a silver moon-painted landing. It was silent, but there were voices, voices as different to the singing as life is to death, as reality is to fantasy.

"She'll be asleep by now. I'll awa' in and set the sock by the foot of the bed."

I was back between the blankets, head on pillow, eyes shut, trying to breathe slowly and quietly, when my blood was away like a run-away horse. I heard the door opening, brushing the carpet . . . heard the stealthy steps, the rustle of cellophane, the in-drawn breath, the steps again, the sigh of the door, the click of the lock. Maggie and May were playing Santa Claus, as they had done before. They could not know the guest they had disturbed, but I knew. I could catch the fragrance of lily-of-the-valley. She had come to me on Christmas morning. Perhaps there was a Jacob's ladder, stretched between heaven and earth in the holiness of Christmas. I had been happy at Old Jethart. The past had blurred at the edges and sometimes, I could not summon up how she had looked, not really clearly, but faintly browning like a photograph. Now the years that were past came down upon me like a cataract. I could see the old living room as if I stood there again . . . see the table set with blue delph, see the sewing machine and the butter-box seat, the rag rugs, the alarm clock on the mantel. I could catch the dirt smell of the stairs past the flat below, almost hear Mrs. Higgins and her breathless voice and the whuff-whuff of her asthma spray. I had allowed happiness to tarnish my memory and perhaps Mother had come back to remind me . . . I turned my face into the pillow and wept, with no thought for the Christmas stocking that Maggie and May had been at such pains to prepare for me, although I was thirteen years old and should have put aside such childish things . . . and so I cried myself asleep and woke next morning and wondered if I had dreamt the whole thing.

Then Christmas was over and Hogmanay too. The new term started in Innish School and the class-room was a place of childblains and cold apples. Johnny McGill was more active with the tawse and Jock McGregor said it was the only way he had of keeping heat in his body. It was not true, for he taught with his back to the fire and often he tapped with his pointer on the brass rail that ran round the wire guard.

My evening lessons with Hamish were far more pleasant and now I tried to please him with all my heart. A word of praise from him was enough to supply a whole day with happiness. In the night, I lay and listened for the song, but it never came. In the whistle of the wind through the sashes, I might imagine I heard singing, but I did not get that feeling as if my Mother stood by my bed . . . nor was I possessed by her spirit with every sense as acute to me as if I lived again in days that were gone.

Yet, I do not know. There was a strange thing happened to me and it was coming up to Easter and perhaps at holy times, there is an easing of such communication. There seems no reason why I should have acted as I did. I was not a reckless child. I was an indifferent horsewoman. It was on Good Friday that I went to the stables to saddle Lady Judy and take her for exercise in the hills. I was wearing my jodhpurs and yellow sweater. The day was mild. I had left off my riding mac and had on my tweed hacking jacket, a tartan scarf tucked into the high neck of my yellow sweater, the yellow string gloves, the jockey cap. I came to Judy's loose box and fed her a lump of sugar and she nuzzled her nose against my pocket and whinnied. Then I went to look over the half door at Sultan. He was standing by the stall with his head down and I watched him for a while and thought what a fine horse he was . . . black as night and handsome. It was a pity that, as Rob said, he had the de'il in him. I had never ridden him, nor was I likely to. He was Cousin David's horse and Hamish could manage him, but he was treacherous. The half light of the stable reminded me of Christmas and I wondered if Christ had really been born in a stable, or if it was all legend . . . the same sort of legend that deepened into mystery at Old Jethart. I remembered Christmas and midnight and the small soft voice. I whistled the air of it through my teeth.

"I had a little nut tree, nothing would it bear . . ."

The horse turned his head to look at me . . . came over to droop his nose over the door. I stroked his ears and he put his soft nostrils against the side of my face and whickered. I went off to the harness room and took his saddle from the rack . . . picked his bridle off its peg . . . came back to the door again and shot the bolt back. In the loose box, the straw smell enclosed me and my fingers were undoing the girth of his blanket, slipping it off, throwing it down on the manger. I was acting like an automaton . . . not half knowing what I was about. The saddle was on his back, the bit in his mouth, the forelock pulled out over the head band. If ever I was compelled to do a thing, it was now, but there was no force . . . no command to be obeyed, just a feeling as if I was drifting along in a course of action, going where my path lead.

Hamish had gone shooting with Rob. Cousin David was away to Oban to fetch tractor spares. Maggie and May were busy in the kitchen. Only Lady Judy watched me from her box, as I led Sultan out into the yard and she seemed willing enough to be left behind. I put a foot in the stirrup and was up on Sultan's back and there was a happiness and a competence about me, as if I had never mounted a horse so gracefully before. I gathered the double reins and well I knew that I would be mistress of my mount. I had a confidence and a strength that I had never experienced before, as I clicked my tongue at him and rode out into the paddock. He went gracefully, into trot, into canter, going in an Arab poetry of motion. I sat in the saddle, a part of him, moving with him, so that we were one. I turned him with rein and knee and he responded, first one way and then another. There was a low wall to the paddock and we flew over it with feet to spare, landing gently in the soft grass of the track to the house. I wondered what miracle had happened, that I felt so much at ease and the answer was clear. I had ridden no steed but Lady Judy and she was no show beast. In my heart, I knew I could compete in any horse show on earth with Sultan. I saw myself with the red rosette in my teeth and heard the crackling applause of the crowd.

We walked quietly up to the front door and stood facing the steps. There seemed no reason to go there, but we went. I wondered what would happen if Maggie or May were to open the door, but anyway I reined up there and stood waiting. I was happy, so happy and the sun was shining . . . God was in heaven and all was right with the world. Then a cloud edged in on the sun and a splash of rain hit my cheek and Sultan was uneasy suddenly and his unease communicated itself to me. By little and by little, my happiness fell away and there was something behind the shut door . . . something that might come out . . . not Maggie nor yet May, but something out of the unknown nowhere . . . out of the same place from whence she had come to sing the song . . . and I remembered the song and was frightened . . . and Sultan wheeled and started to trot quickly away from the house. I was not afraid he would throw me . . . not afraid of being on his back. I could manage horses far more difficult than he. I turned him into the avenue and he answered my rein. I kicked my heels against his side and he cantered, galloped. We went down the grass of the avenue and over a post and rail fence and along the side of the ten-acre field, faster and faster and faster again, faster than ever horse had raced before and there was no horse born that could catch us and I was safe . . . for there were those, that came after me. My scarf blew out of the neck of my sweater and flew like a tartan banner behind me and the rain was lashing down in earnest now, but we cared nothing for it. I bent down along Sultan's neck and heard the whip of the scarf and the beat of the hooves softened against the turf. We were on the path to the sea, where horses were never taken, but I did not care where we went. I knew that I could ride for ever on this horse, over hedge and wall and bank, ride on to happiness without end . . . yet still there was this shadow, that followed us in the flash of lightning . . . and the roll of thunder . . . and I was not Belinda McLean, but a woman without fear. There was no leash of terror to hold me back and I faced Sultan at a five barred gate and we were over it and my laughter was scattered on the wind. It seemed to go on for ever. There was a sheep track under our feet and hungry sea grass and the bit was between his teeth and he was away now and I lay along his neck and laughed at the headland and the cliff and the knowledge that the sea was five hundred feet below . . . Now, I knew this was the place they called the Leap. Maybe somebody had told me of it, maybe not, but I knew. You could jump a horse from the top of the cliff into eternity and live out the end of your life in happiness . . . for ever and ever and ever . . . with all sadness gone to oblivion and all problems solved . . . you could ride your horse across the sky . . .

I came to my senses twenty yards from the top of the cliff and remembered who I was, realised where I was, hardly comprehended how I came to be there. I had had some sort of a fugue . . . I had sleep-walked in the day and my feet had brought me to death. Two more bounds and I would rise into the air like Pegasus for the crash to the rocks below. Then there was a shout and Hamish leapt for the rein. I saw him for a split moment as he came out from behind a boulder right in my path. He grabbed the bridle in his hand and we slithered, haunch-skidded and slid and maybe I screamed, or maybe the wind shrilled. My eyes were tight shut in that second and when I opened them, I was on the edge of the cliff and it was crumbling away under the horse's hooves and he was shinnying and backing, backing, backing . . . and Hamish was gone over the cliff. Then Rob was there with his face waxen throwing down his gun to grab the reins and I was off the horse and down on the grass, edging out to look and there was a feeling of evil and hate and horror . . . such horrors as I had never known . . . and of tears and parting and heartbreak and torment. Then calm and the sight of Hamish caught on a mountain ash a little way down the cliff.

I stretched my hand out but he was ten feet below me and my weight was crumbling earth and sand down on him and Rob was shouting at me to get back and I was screaming that Hamish was there. I could see the sea far off below and my senses spun with the awfulness of it and his face was bleeding ... He had let go of the rowan branch and was seeking for handholds and footholds and the sea creamed and churned. Then Rob was at my side his hands cupped to his mouth.

"Are ye all right laddie?"

Another shower of earth and sand went down and blinded Hamish and he clung there and cursed in fine Highland words that were whipped out of his mouth by the wind.

"Get back from there. You'll have the whole cliff down on top of me. Is that damned girl out of her mind, Rob? For God's sake, take her out of there ... see to the horse ..."

Inch by inch, he crept up the face of the scree, and sometimes he slipped back and hung between life and death and I lay full length on the grass and watched him and as he came closer I saw there was no fear in him, only a fine rage, that made nothing of his peril.

"Why didn't you throw yourself out of the saddle?" he yelled at me, his face near enough to mine and the blood making runnels down his forehead and dripping on his chest. I got my handkerchief out of my pocket and tried to wipe it but he turned away from me, told me to let him be, that I had done enough mischief already. Then the handkerchief blew away and went spiralling slowly down and down, so that I was giddy watching it, till I could see it no more against the foam and the white spume of the waves.

He had a knee over the edge now and Rob had his shoulder and was heaving him up, but he threw off Rob's help too and got to his feet, took me by the elbow and dragged me back six yards. Sultan was grazing by the boulder with the reins in a tangle and Hamish went to disentangle them and threw them over his head, stood there with his hand on the curb chain, glaring at me.

"Have you any explanation?"

"I don't know . . . I don't know . . . I don't know."

"Maybe you wanted to see the Leap?" he said and there was a knife in his voice and a hot hatred of me.

I sat down on the grass, for my legs went under me like feathers and when I looked at him again, he was staring out to sea.

"If that's the way of it, you got your wish," he said. "There's the famous leap, where I just climbed up, and yourself no help at all, but to throw half the cliff into my eyes. Your Aunt Con was killed at this very spot, or didn't they tell you that? There's a lot they haven't told you, isn't there? She travelled the same path you travelled, but she didn't care if she lived or if she died, with the love she had for David . . . and he with no sense in his head. Maybe you don't know that he didn't look the side of the road Con was on, with the love he had for your mother. Con went over the cliff there and she had no rowan to break her fall. They got her up on ropes with a stretcher, smashed to hell and all her beauty gone . . . smashed to hell, as you might have been smashed to hell . . ."

He put his foot in the stirrup and got into the saddle as stiffly as an old man, turned the horse's head towards home and looked back at me over his shoulder.

"You're not to tell what happened here today. Tell any lie you like, but don't tell him that your horse bolted and took you near over the Leap. He's not to know that. There's no point in . . . Oh, to blazes with it! You wanted to ride Sultan and he bolted with you. I stopped you just down the avenue near the gate and that's how I got my scratches. He's not to know you came anywhere within the bawl of an ass of this place. There's nobody in the parish will come next or near it. There's a story about it and I never believed it, but I did today, when

I saw your face. It was God's mercy that Rob and I came this way. I clapped eyes on you when you were almost at the edge. There was death in your face, if ever I saw death. You might have had a host of Sutherlands at your back with drawn swords in their hands . . . and now good day to you . . ."

He wheeled the horse and was gone at a full gallop and I put my head in my hands and gave myself up to misery. Rob came over and his hand was kind on my hair.

"Don't greet, lassie. Ye should be thanking yer Maker."

"I'm not greeting, Rob."

I remembered the same sort of scene the day Mother had died.

"I'm not crying, sir. No more you are, ducks . . ."

"I couldn't help it. Something got into me. I went out to the stable to put the saddle on Judy and it wasn't me any more. I could ride like I've never ridden before. I can't explain . . . I don't know what possessed me . . ."

"If ye'd ha' seen yoursel' coming down yon cliff with the tartan stole streaming out behind ye, ye'd ha' known what possessed ye."

He spat into the dead bracken and helped me to my feet.

"We'd best get walkin', for there are three hard miles betwixt us and hame."

He told me as we went along, the legend of the Leap, the legend of the ancient curse. It had all happened a long time ago, before the house was built. There was another house, stood where it stood now and its name "Old Jethart" and the Sutherlands lived there, a family with "six braw sons" but the ain lassie, her that's in the painting ower the dining-room mantel.

She loved "the black McLean" and he loved her, but the Sutherlands would have none of him. The loves planned a runaway marriage. It was Lord Ullin's daughter all over again.

"He cam' in the nicht to fetch her awa' . . . wi' his steed at the front door and the wind rising sairly..."

He swung her up on the saddle in front of him and away, but the brothers poured down the steps after them, with swords in their hands and now it was "Young Lochinvar" and his fair Ellen.

There was a chase along the sea and a confrontation at the top of the headland... at the very edge of the cliff.

It was the stuff of such Scots legends, but I knew what she had felt, the lady in the painting.

"Ye'll no pairt us," McLean had yelled. "We'll gae together and I'll pit a fine curse on ye, 'fore I gae."

It was to last down the years, the curse of black McLean and it was early death for all Sutherlands... and their loved ones.

"If I canna live oot my life wi' my loved lassie, then nane who cam' aifter, will dae it..."

Rob had studied it well and he believed it every word. He knew the curse off by heart and he declaimed it with a fine Scots mein.

"There'll be no happiness in Old Jethart till a black McLean shall come, who will stand on this place, where noo I stand ... to forgive the wrang ye dae tae me and then do penance by exile frae bonnie Scotland, till the sin is wiped oot..." Then he turned his horse's face to the sea and he leaped to his death for neither he nor his bride were ever seen again.

"My Father came here and took Mother away, Rob," I mused. "If the legend is right, he might have broken the curse. If he had gone out to the Leap and said he forgave the Sutherlands, it might have worked, but it all seems impossible. It hasn't done the family much harm, has it?"

He stopped up short at that and looked at me with amazement, asked me if I had been in the graveyard to look at the tomb "stanes". In my own time, my Mother who was a Sutherland, and her good man, her sister, Constance, the finest horse woman in Scotland. David's father and his mother, his grandfather and grandmother . . . and so on.

"Mr. Hamish kenn't it was true today, when he saw ye riding tae the cliff top."

The darkness was coming down and the stars were pale in the sky. It was the gloaming, a time when you might believe the impossible. My mother had come to me at Christmas and sung her song, but today, there had been another "manifestation" that the dead slept uneasily. I half believed it. It was not myself who had taken Sultan from his stable. I could never have ridden him in such a way. I had not the ability and I had not the nerve. Somebody had taken possession of me and I thought there were two possibilities. It might have been Aunt Con, but again, she herself might have been "possessed" by a more powerful spirit. There was the lady in the painting. If I swallowed the whale of Scots legend, why should I strain at the gnat? The moon was misty, a crescent moon with a star at its tip. It might be that the lady in the painting had possessed Aunt Con, as she possessed me . . . might have taken her to her death.

"Why did Aunt Constance ride out to the Leap, Rob?"

He could never understand it . . . none of them could. She was a fine rider and the horse would never have got the better of her.

"But Hamish said she did it because she loved Cousin David . . . that she meant to do it."

"Hamish says mair than his prayers. Mistress Con was a member of the kirk and she said her prayers every day. She'd as soon jump into heil fire, as tak' her ain life."

"But Cousin David loved Mother?"

"Maybe aye, maybe no."

He led the horse into the stable yard and put him in the loose-box, hung a fresh hay-bag on the hook, set about taking off the harness, while I busied myself with the feed next door.

I tilted the fodder into the manger and he watched me out of the corner of his eye.

"The bluid of the McLeans runs in yer ain veins, lassie . . . but that's not all. Ye hae the bluid of the Sutherlands frae yer mither's side. It cam' intae ma heid just noo, that mebbe ye were sent to Old Jethart wi' a purpose . . ."

110

PART FOUR

The months slipped by. The lambs appeared like lost wool scarves on the mountains. The primroses bloomed and the cowslips, the violets. The heather turned the hills to purple and then in no time at all, there were berries on the rowans and the bracken was setting the countryside aflame with the fiery cross of its dying. Then the snow capped the mountains and the Christmas tree was brought into the hall, I did not know that I held an hour-glass in my hand and that the sand had almost all run out. I was spending the last of my childhood at Old Jethart.

I had not unravelled the full mystery of the house, nor was it likely that I should. Maggie watched me put on my new white dress for supper on Christmas day and as I draped the tartan stole with the white fringed edge across my shoulder, she told me that I might have stood for the painting of the lady in the dining room downstairs.

"It's just the white dress and the bright scarf," I said. "She's not like me in the face and her hair's fair."

Darkness had fallen and we had been telling ghost stories, as we baked the chestnuts on the bars of the grate in the sitting room. The eeriness hung about us still and Maggie looked across at me, her face as serious as it had been half an hour since, when she assured us all that there was a gentleman in old-fashioned dress, all green, that haunted the Manse. It seemed that the Bishop had woken up in bed one time and found "the green man" standing at his side, and had got a terrible fright, had got up and packed his bags, had quitted Innish within the hour.

"Ellen Sutherland, her in the dining room below, is supposed to walk the landing outside the door there."

"So her name is 'Ellen' and that's about right, for there's a touch of Lochinvar in the tale," I laughed. "I daresay Auld Rob sees her looking out of the window and down at the flight of stairs on his way home to bed on a Saturday's night, when he's 'fu' like Robbie Burns's heroes."

I felt a shiver along my spine all the same, for I was still in the mood for tales of mystery and imagination.

"I thought I saw her walk there myself a time or two. I dinna like to think of it, for she walks, when a tragedy strikes the place. I saw her the night before your Aunt Con went to her death from the cliffs. Maybe I was dreaming, but something lifted me from my bed and made me open my door and I thought I saw her in front of me . . . not walking, kind o' floating along the corridor. When she got gin the window, she vanished . . ."

There was a troubled look on her face, that did not match the gay atmosphere of the white dress, new from Jenner's in Edinburgh, did not match the glory of the tartan stole and the big Caingorn brooch . . .

"I have na' told anybody . . . not May even, for she's easy filled wi' alarm . . . and you profess not to believe such tales, but I saw her again last night, hinny . . . or maybe it was the moon throwing down wairse shadows through the glass."

The small hairs were standing on the nape of my neck by now, as they had been for an hour by the sitting room fire and my face blazing hot from roasting chestnuts. I sat down on the stool and tied the ribbon round the plait on my right hand side, set it near my ear . . . turned my attention to the other side and watched her in the mirror over the dressing table.

"Did *you* hear anything last night?" she asked.

I tried to bring back the carnival feeling and told her that if I had heard anything, I would have thought it was May and herself playing Father Christmas when we were all getting a bit adult for such games. Then I decided that I might confide in her. I looked at the comfortable dumpling figure and the familiar white starched apron, up to the dimpled chin and the blue eyes.

"I'm not laughing at you really. I'm whistling in the dark, Maggie, for one time, I thought I heard my mother here. It was very real and it almost broke my heart. She was singing in a strange little voice and I smelt the lily-of-the-valley scent. The door swung shut and she was gone. Do you think that she did come to my bed that night?"

She moved to the stool and took my head against her side and called me her poor wee lamb and I went on and told her that it had been Christmas then too, and I had thought of a Jacob's ladder . . . and how at Easter, when it was holy time again, I had been possessed enough to ride the horse out to the Leap.

"Nobody knows about it, only Hamish and Rob. It's not to be told to Cousin David on any account, but there's a mystery about Old Jethart and it's possible that there are spirits, which still . . . which still . . . I don't know . . . stay haunting and waiting maybe . . ."

She scolded me about riding Sultan, possessed or not, told me I was possessed with the de'il, then she nodded her white head and her face was unlike itself . . . a face I had never seen. So it must have looked when tragedy hit the house and it had struck again and again in Maggie's lifetime.

"You're old enough to think on such things, hinny. I didn't think you were, yet a while, but I've always felt Old Jethart is fu' of other beings, not just you and me and Mr. David, but gentle people, who come and go. There's times, where a door opens with no hand to open it, and a creak of the stair when no foot treads. Your Aunt Con and your mother . . . they were the most beautiful lassies in the kingdom, as like as two peas in a pod, height and colour and face and carriage and voice. If you were to pass one of them on the landing, you'd look back to see which it was. Your mother was aye laughing and Con was serious, but they were like one soul, shared out betwixt two bodies . . . and the love . . . the love. Maybe they shared the love too, but that's neither here nor there. It was like David and Jonathan, but death parted them . . . Auld Rob has it that there's girls' voices and laughing in the night, but he's a wee bit fey, as you ken. We don't take overmuch notice of him, but an odd time, I've heard somebody laughing . . and now that you say it, I've heard singing and said to myself that it's the wind in the sashes . . ."

"But if you saw the lady of the portrait last night, Maggie, that means trouble for the house?"

The sad mood had gone on too long. I saw it in the forced cheerfulness of her face, which dimpled back to its old calm happiness.

"If the place is so fu' of ghosts, the dear knows who I saw . . . and now, enough of this nonsensical carrying on . . . We're no better than Auld Rob in the kitchen below, keeping his eye on the punch sauce . . . Get along with you downstairs, for Mister David will have his eyes worn out watching for you in your new frock."

I ran off across the room, thinking that she had said that Mother shared "love" with Aunt Con and that might mean her love of Cousin David. Maggie had considered ours an important conversation, for all she made light of it. I watched her through the evening and there was a shade of sadness against the festivity of Christmas Day. As for Cousin David, he got to his feet as I came into the room and held out his hand to me and his words brought my mother back to stand at my side again.

"Och, you're a bonnie lassie grown," he smiled. "You're more like your mother with every day that passes. I sometimes see you coming across a room and think she's come back to Old Jethart to haunt me to my grave."

It was strange in the light of what followed, what happened that Christmas Day. I was to think of it again and again in the years that followed. Of course, she had loved him . . . had loved him all the time and run off in a romantic elopement, that had run short of romance. I had only to will myself back to the old rooms in the tenement. When she had spoken of him, her spirit had come alive. I had thought it was Old Jethart, but it was David Sutherland. I was almost sure of it. My father must have come to be sure of it too . . . and taken to the dram to live with the truth of what he found out.

At any rate, that day, I listened to Cousin David's words with a pricking of my thumbs. I ran across the room and put my arms about his neck to hug him. We were alone together and my passion for Hamish was a different emotion from what I felt for Cousin David, who was my whole world.

"I love you," I told him. "I love you better than all the universe put together. If you had been my real father, I could never have loved you as I do at this moment."

I bounced out of his arms and went to sit on the rug at his feet with my arms hugging my knees.

"I've come to a decision these last few days. I'll not marry anyone . . ."

Hamish had been like flint to me, for the eight months since my escapade on the cliff, I had decided that he might "never look the side of the road I was on". Another girl might have thought of taking the veil, but I had other plans.

"I'm never going to get married, so you needn't be thinking I'll leave you lonely in Old Jethart. In two years time, I'll be turned sixteen and Maggie will let me put my hair up. For the rest of my days, till it's as white as snow, I'll sit at the foot of your table and see after you and love you, 'till all the seas gang dry . . .'"

He laughed at my earnest face and told me that "the best laid schemes of mice and men gang aft agley" and perhaps he looked into the future or perhaps he did not. I was glad of the way the day turned out, very glad of it in the days that followed . . . and I wondered if Mother had put the words into my mouth to say I would love him till "all the seas gang dry".

So Christmas Day passed by and we were happy, very happy indeed, but there was no happy new years at our feet.

It was the day after, on St. Stephen's day, that the whole of my ivory tower tumbled about my ears. It was a cold frosty day and Hamish wanted to go shooting. Cousin David said that he was far too lazy. He had eaten too much at lunchtime and he was going to play chess with me in front of the sitting room fire. Hamish looked sulky at that and said "Very well, then," with an ill grace and Cousin David said that he would go out for an hour. He went off upstairs and changed into his shooting gear and he collected his twelve-bore gun from the gun rack in the hall and came back to the fire. Maggie had washed my hair in soft rain water an hour before and I was sitting on the hearthrug, combing it out. It curled all down my shoulders to my waist and he picked up a strand of it.

"It's nice to think of you sitting at my fire, waiting for me to come back," he said, as he stooped to kiss the top of my head. "You're a nice lassie to come home to and I'll be no longer than I can help. Do you set out the chessmen on the board and I'll be back before you miss me."

I set the board up on the table and stood the pieces in position. Then I brushed my hair, twisted it into two plaits, tried out new hair styles. I arranged it in a chignon on the nape of my neck and looked at myself in the mirror and I got out a lipstick, that Maggie did not know I had, and put on a very red mouth. After a while, I changed the style. I wound the plaits round my head like a coronet, but I did not like it like that, so I piled it all up on the top, and thought I was wonderfully fashionable.

I heard footsteps scrunching on the drive and wondered who it was and in ten seconds, the sitting room door burst open and sprung back against the wall with a crash. I jumped to my feet in alarm and saw Hamish, his face as white as a ghost's and his eyes staring out of his head.

"Oh, God!" he said. "Oh, God!"

He said it over and over again.

"Oh, God! Oh, God!"

He walked stiffly across the carpet, like an old man, leaned his head on his arms on the mantelpiece.

"Oh, God! Oh, God!" he said over and over and over.

I had sent the chessmen all over the floor in my fright.

"What happened?" I asked him, my voice croaking, but he took no notice of me, and my heart was thudding against my ribs.

I grasped his shoulder and shook him. I turned him round to face me and he was like a man in a dream of death. He raised his head slowly and his eyes lifted to mine and he said "What will become of you now? Oh, God? What will become of Maggie and Auld Rob?"

"It's Cousin David?" I whispered and he nodded his head.

"Is he dead?" I asked him and my child's voice echoed in every corner of the room. It was as if I had thrown a pebble into a pool and the sound spread ripples all through the house.

"Dead, dead, dead, dead, dead..."

He nodded slowly and the walls moved in to close down on me.

"The gun went off..." he said, in a dreadful automatic way, as if he were frozen up in the horror of it. "He got the full charge in the chest at point blank range... He was climbing through the hedge at the bottom of the hill, where the bramble bushes are thick. He's down there now . . . all alone. I shouldn't have left him alone, should I?" I tried to say something, but I had no voice. I was dumb with the shock of it. Yet here I was, back on the ceiling again, in the old terrible way, floating along like a child's lonely lost balloon, waiting to see what would happen . . . watching to see what I would do and say. I saw myself pick up the telephone and look at it for a long time and then I heard myself speaking to the doctor.

"This is Belinda, from Old Jethart. There's been a terrible accident. Could you please come quickly? It's Cousin David. He's been killed."

I saw myself cross to Hamish and put my arms about him. I led him to a chair and sat on the arm of it and his black head was on my breast.

"It was all my fault. We changed guns. I thought mine was firing to the right . . . I cocked it ready for him . . . But nothing got up. I shouldn't have cocked it. It was my fault the brambles weren't cut back. He told me last week to see to it, and I had put it off, because we were getting ready for Christmas. My God! He didn't want to come out shooting today and I made him. He was afraid I would be jealous of the attention he gave to you . . . always. I showed him today that I was jealous. I was black dour on purpose to force him to come with me and not stay with you! I was like a senseless bairn. He wanted to turn back and come home to you and I told him there was a bird on the hill. It was a bloody lie. There weren't any birds there. I wanted him to try my gun . . . Oh, God! I wish I was down there instead of him, flung on the grass, with my heart shot out of my chest. He was worth twenty thousand of me. He took me into his home, when I was a wee laddie with none to want me . . . not a penny piece in the world. He treated me like a favourite son. I'm a Jonah! I kill everybody I love . . . Father and Mother and now David . . . David . . .

David... Oh, God! Oh, God!"

I kissed his cold cheek and told him to stop talking nonsense. It was an accident, I said. It was Cousin David's duty to see that the gun was on the safety catch. He knew it was cocked and anyhow, he always broke the gun, getting through a hedge. He always lectured us about doing that. He just forgot this one time. It was nobody's fault and he was not to blame himself for it.

"It was my fault. If I had shot him down with my own hand, I couldn't be more to blame. Why didn't I put the catch on the gun? Why didn't I let him come home, when he wanted to? Oh, God! Why didn't I?"

I stayed up on the ceiling and watched my body walk down the hall to the kitchen to break the news to Maggie and May. I felt nothing up there, as I watched the flood tide of grief washing the happiness out of the house. I watched them bringing him home up the six shallow steps on a field gate and still I could not cry. His face was very handsome, as he lay in his bed in the room upstairs, with my Christmas roses by his hand. The dark lashes were down on his white cheeks and his hair shone silver in the dim light of the room. I kissed his cold cheek and it was colder than any stone. I sat in the front pew in the Church and saw his coffin beside me in the aisle, with my wreath on his breast and I still could not weep. It was worse than Mother's death had been. I had loved him just as much as ever I had loved her and I thought that my life had ended with his. I saw the coffin go down into the cold earth and a little East wind was shrilling about the tombstones, and under the tombstones about, his kin all dead too soon. There was a feeling of snow in the air and a white icing on every one of the silent mountains around us. I threw the bunch of the first snowdrops down on the lid of the coffin and saw the name plate shine up at me. I heard the earth thudding on it and saw the tears run down the faces of Maggie and May. I heard the skirl of the pipes in the lament and it tore my heart to shreds. I put out a hand to find Hamish's hand and remembered that they had taken him away in the doctor's car that awful afternoon and he was still in the hospital, off his head with grief. I walked back to Old Jethart with the Minister beside me and he told me that I was a brave little lassie. He said that I must not weep for my Cousin David, who was not dead, but only gone ahead, to a far better and a brighter land.

I turned to the Minister.

"If God is trying to persuade Cousin David that Heaven is happier than Old Jethart was with Hamish and me, he'll have no success," I said and he looked shocked.

"You mustn't talk like that, Belinda," he scolded me. "There's no place happier or better than the next world. He'll be at rest there and at peace, wi' all his ain folk, who have gone before him."

I had tea in the sitting room with the Minister and his wife and with the Dominie and I don't know whom else. Maggie and May brought in tea for the ladies and whisky for the gentlemen and people kept coming up to me to say how sorry they were and what a good man Cousin David had been. I could have told them how good he had been. I answered politely and poured out the tea and Maggie and May passed the cups and the glasses round, their eyes red from weeping. It all went on for ever and ever. I felt nothing at all even yet. My feelings were pack ice inside my breast. I knew that the pain would come melting in soon, till my whole being was just desolation and loneliness.

The solicitor stayed on, when the others had gone. I smelt the whisky on his breath and knew that he had drunk a lot of it. He sat in David's place at the head of the dining room table and I had supper with him and we carried on a polite conversation. I suppose he was used to such things.

It had been a very cold day for the funeral, hadn't it? Indeed it had, and the wind lay in the east, which meant more snow at this time of the year. It was very early for snowdrops. Where had I managed to find some? Maggie always put down a pane of glass over a sheltered place in the garden, and we always had them for Christmas . . . on the table for Christmas dinner, but this year, we had had Christmas roses . . . the same ones, that were there now. Oh, God! How could it be possible? Did I like Scotland better than London? Oh, yes, of course, I loved it here. Even the school? He had heard that Johnny McGill was over-generous with the tawse. I liked the school fine and the Dominie was always fair. You were never punished unless you deserved it. The conversation went on and on and on and then supper was over and my head was aching.

We went across the hall to sit in the sitting room and Maggie brought in the coffee for me to pour out and handed round the small cups and I thought how big the solicitor's nose looked, when he drunk out of his.

"When you and May are cleared away," he said to Maggie. "I'd thank you to come in here, for what I have to say concerns you all and I may tell you now that it's not good news."

Maggie and May came in presently and settled themselves down side by side on the sofa, and I went and fetched the brief case for the solicitor from the hall. He took some papers out of it and adjusted his gold rimmed glasses on his nose. He cleared his throat and told us that the estate had been mortgaged . . . heavily mortgaged.

"You all knew about it perhaps, but in case you did not, I will tell you that Mr. Sutherland took out a mortgage to the full value of the property after the death of your father, Belinda. You may know that he was deeply in love with your mother, now deceased, and he had hoped that she would come to him for aid. However, she was a proud lassie, and she made no communication of any sort to him, although he advertised so widely that she must have seen his insertions. He left the farm and searched the whole country for her, but with no success, and she had no way of knowing that he was ruining himself, in the hopeless seekings for her. He was very much in love with her and I have always been convinced that she loved him too, but she was over proud to come, as she would have thought, begging to his door."

I clenched my hands in my lap and dug the nails into my palms, as he went on "He returned after a few years, a most unhappy man, and his fortunes never recovered. He had a large interest to pay off every year and had no chance whatever of repaying the loan. The bank will foreclose on the entire estate."

I thought that it could not be happening to me. I could not be hearing that there was nothing left of all the lovely place. It must be nightmare and in a moment I would wake up.

"However, there are some items, which we must save from the ruin. I think that there would be no objection on the part of the bank if we let his cousin, Hamish Sutherland inherit his personal jewellery . . . his gold watch, a half hunter, and another watch for the wrist, also gold."

He settled his glasses more comfortably on his nose, and went on, "his signet rings and his Mother's wedding ring, and various items of minor interest."

It could not be Cousin David's things he was talking about in this bread-and-butter way . . . without a smile or a tear or a sigh . . . not the gold half-hunter, that he wore riding, and took out to look at, when it was time to come home again . . . not the signet ring, that had gleamed on his finger every day of his life. I used to turn it round sometimes, if I held his hand and once or twice, he put it on me for fun, to see how small my fingers were.

"There is a special bequest for you, Belinda." He took up the brief case again and lifted out a narrow wrapped parcel, sealed with red wax.

"Before that however, I had better give you this."

He handed a wisp of tissue paper into my hand and I opened it up. A lock of black glossy hair gleamed in the light.

"It's a lock of your mother's hair, on which he put great sentimental value. He kept it on him, everywhere he went and he wanted you to have it when he was dead."

Why had no one prepared me for the frightful anguish, that took me in the heart like a spear, when I looked down at the black curl of hair . . . as black as ebony . . . as black as night . . . as black as my own black plaits, that hung down each of my shoulders? I felt I must die, with the sorrow, that flooded in upon me, and I was no child's lost balloon now, but he went on with my torture, handing me the wrapped parcel, which I undid, knowing that I would find the white book, that I knew so well.

"The entire estate was to be divided equally between Hamish and you, Belinda, but of course, you realise, there is nothing to divide. I was to give this book into your hand and to say to you, that it is entirely due to your very dear self, that his broken heart was put together again quite perfectly and that he died a happy man."

I opened the book at the old familiar place and glanced at the last line of all and knew that it was true for him. I knew he had found his Mary Stuart by now. I excused myself very politely and calmly, saying that I wanted to fetch something from my room, and I ran up the stairs and lay across my bed and wept hard, bitter tears, that tore my chest and throat, till I thought I should die for the agony I felt. I pulled myself together presently and sponged my face and went back to find the solicitor still busy with his papers. As I came into the room, Maggie walked across to meet me and took me into her arms, with the tears streaming down her old face spotting the white apron and her hair shining in the light, her voice very Scots, in her distress.

"He says ye'll have to go, hinny. There's nae money to support ye and naebody tae tend ye. May and I wid hae ye and welcome, but he says that's not good enough, for we'll hae tae work for our living. He says that ye'll hae to gae to the Childrens' Home, as soon as we've finished up here and ye'll be there, till ye come o' age in four years and then ye'll be yer own mistress and dae whit ye please. Dear God! If Master David were tae see this day, his hairt would be broken all ower again."

I sat down in my chair at last and heard the solicitor tell me that he was very sorry, but he had no option but to inform the County Council, that I was in need of care and protection and must be taken under their wing within the next week or so, as soon as Old Jethart was shut up.

It was a dreadful week . . . that last week. I will never forget the black desolation of it, if I live to be an old woman. Maggie and May and I cleared up the whole house. We packed Cousin David's clothes carefully and went through all his private things. I learned to hold myself ready for the spears of pain which pierced me again and again, when I came on some familiar thing. I found the red velvet dress that he had bought for me in Jenner's on my first morning in Scotland . . . my letter to him from England . . . a lock of my hair, the picture of me winning the jumping competition on Lady Judy at the Show . . . a letter from Johnny McGill, to tell him that I was a bright lassie and ask about the possibility of Edinburgh University in a few years time . . . a dreadful letter from Mother to him, written on the night of her elopement with Father . . . these and a hundred other things which brought him back again before eyes, that burned from my tears, that would not seem to stop, now that they had begun to flow.

The last evening of all, I was sitting in the study, as miserable as I could possibly be, tying up the books into bundles for the auction next week. The furniture was all stuck with red numbers and the carpet was rolled up at the side of the room.

Even the clock was silent, as if time had stopped for me, as indeed it had. Hamish was still in the hospital and was allowed no visitors. He was expected to be there for six months and had not been told of our present plight. I had had my tea in the kitchen with Maggie and May, but none of us had eaten anything. They worried about me all the time and tried to make hopeful plans for my future. They would find another job and save their money... every bit of it. Maggie was due to retire in two or three years and they would rent that small cottage down the road from the gates of Old Jethart. May would go out to any work she could get as a daily maid and Maggie would have the pension. It would be enough for the three of us, if we were careful. It was the best we could hope for. I was due to go to the Childrens' Home the next morning at nine. I was to be called for by a Miss Burns... a Childrens' Officer, in her blue Ford Prefect. She had thrown out a dreadful hint this morning to Maggie and we had been able to think of nothing else the whole day. The local Home was being closed in a month or two. I was an English child. I might be sent back to my birthplace as their responsibility. My mind shied away from the thought, as Lady Judy shied from a tuft of grass if the mood was on her. I could not even bring myself to think of the possibility of leaving Scotland. There was not one bright cloud in the whole sky, as far as I could see.

I did not hear Auld Rob come into the room, till he stood by my side. I had not turned on the light, but had worked in the glow of the peat fire and he appeared as silently as a ghost.

"They tell me, ye'r awa the morn?" he said, and went over to look down into the fire.

It lit up his lined face, his piercing eagle's eyes, his big Scots nose, his sunken mouth, his tattered tweed jacket, his tartan kilt, the gay tam o' shanter, that had wiped the tears from his eyes by the grave.

"Maggie's greetin' in the kitchen, that ye'll be awa' tae England maybe. Ye're awa' to the Hame tomorrow, and 'tis like ye'll go to your ain toon in the ... south."

I said nothing and he turned and looked at me like a hawk, so fierce and bright was his eye.

"It came tae me, that a McLean's tae gae tae exile," he said, his voice was so low, as to be almost a whisper.

I thought that he was trying to make a joke to cheer me up. I tried to manage a smile, but I failed to do anything but bare my teeth at him.

"A black McLean! Wi' hair like a corbie's wing."

He was talking about the superstition. He had not talked about anything else to me, for eight-nine months.

"It seems tae me that the two hundred years arc up," he said. "Ye've but to cam' oot to yon cliff with me noo, and say ye forgive the Sutherlands for the wrang they did the McLeans, and the evil will be lifted frae this hoose, and the last mon of them a', can live to a ripe old age wi' his bonny bride."

"Don't be foolish, Rob! Hamish is away from here now and no Sutherland is likely to buy the place. The curse won't reach them now."

"Ye dinna have to live at Old Jethart to dee," he said, with his sly grin.

"Oh, Rob!" I cried in despair. "Please don't worry me with anything else. I can't bear it. Go away and let me finish my work."

"Ye think it's daft," he said and went back to look into the fire again. "Whit aboot the Laird dead and he not near forty yet .. him, that should hae lived till he was ower three score years and ten. It's no' daft, Mistress McLean, and I'll thank ye to come wi' me, for I've borrowed the Minister's lady's mare, since our ain are gane. I hae her ootside the door and you can ride to the Leap, wi' me by yer side."

I sat down on a chair and put my head in my arms on the

table and I wished I were dead. If I went there at all, it would be to jump down to an escape from my sorrow.

"Go away".

"I'll no' gang awa'," he told me calmly. "Not till ye cam' wi' me. I thought ye were a brave lassie, without a fear in yer breast, like yer mither before ye. It seems that ye'r content to have set yoursel' on a cushion and takken a' the soft livin' the Laird poured oot on ye, without a thought of paying him back. He gave you all your hairt desired and noo, ye'll not tak' the curse frae his hoose, and he in his grave."

I wondered if Cousin David would want me to walk out in the dark at this time of night with this half-crazy old man and knew he would have forbidden it.

"Mr. Hamish will dee in a few days, if ye dinna gae."

"Oh, no! Oh, no!"

"If ye dinna gae wi' me noo," he said seriously, coming over to look straight into my eyes. "If ye dinna gae, I swear before the Almighty, that Mr. Hamish will lie beside the Laird within the next month."

I looked at him and felt the doubts clouding my mind, like the mist that comes up from the sea in the evening.

"I've seen it here for seventy years, Mistress. My first maister and his guid wife . . . his son and his wife . . . your father, your mither, your Auntie Constance, and the young laird oot there in his last bed, wi' the flowers no' withered on it. If ye draw back noo, Mr. Hamish will lie beside him, before the moon's fu' agen, and ye'll come back again yersel' to lie beside the baith o' them, too soon, for ye've Sutherland bluid in yer veins from the very branch of them with the curse on their heids."

"I'm not dressed to ride a horse," I said.

"I've the side saddle on the mare. Ye can put on a warm coat and sit on that as soft as if ye were in a chair by the peat fire. I'll keep my hand on the bridle. Ye needn't be feert."

"What do you think I'm afraid of?" I asked him suddenly. "I'm not afraid of death. If I am one of the cursed ones, then the sooner I'm gone, the better for me."

"Ye're destined for happiness, hinny," he smiled suddenly, seeing I was coming with him. "Dinna think the whole lang year is dark, because of ain dark nicht. The sun will rise for ye and ye'll be happy agen and laugh agen."

When I think back on it now, it seems quite impossible that I ever made that moonlight walk with Auld Rob. It did not seem real to me at the time. He led the mare out of the stable and lifted me to her back and then he took her bridle to lead me out of the yard. The moon was at the full and the whole house was silvered and beautiful in the light. It was a cold frosty night and the mare's hooves made a sharp ringing sound against the cobbles. Auld Rob strode on at a good pace and we soon got clear of the house and yard and came out into the open fields. The sky was brilliant with stars and I wondered if it were really possible that Cousin David was in his grave and that I was to leave Old Jethart tomorrow. It was a dreadful dream and soon I must wake in my brass bedstead, warm and comfortable, with the moon shining in through the window to sigh with relief and turn over to sleep again. We did not talk to each other, Auld Rob and I, he picked his way over the rough places, as sure-footed as the mare was, and I clung to the pommel of the saddle and tried to ease my instep from the rubbing of the stirrup and prayed that I might wake up. It seemed to last for ever. It was a lifetime till we came out on the slope to the cliff edge. I looked at the sky again, as we came to the last fifty yards before the Leap and saw that there were small clouds liks wisps of muslin floating across the moon and that the clouds were coming up in a heavy bank on the horizon and would soon blind the beauty of the night.

I felt the horse stop and Rob's hand come up to lift me down.

"What do I do?" I asked him and shivered in the cold breeze, that had sprung up and was coming straight in from the sea, bringing the clouds.

He seemed at a loss what to do himself. It was an eerie place in the bright moonlight and he was afraid. He voiced my thoughts directly.

"The whole air is fu' o' them," he muttered to himself. "There's ghaisties and sperrits a' aboot our heids."

I might have been terrified at another time, but I did not care what became of me now.

"What do I do?" I asked him again.

"Ye tell them ye forgive them," he said, twitching at the mare's bridle.

I went out to the very edge of the cliff and wished I had the courage to step off it. There was a silver path across the sea and I wondered if I could walk across it and come to Cousin David again.

I lifted my arms in front of me.

"Black McLean!" I shouted and my voice was thin and seemed a pale sound in the vastness of the sky and the sea. "Black McLean! Are you listening?"

"For God's sake, lassie. Dinna call him like that. Whit if he were to answer ye?"

"If you're there, McLean," I yelled, but the voice was shrunk in my mouth by the shrilling of the wind over the cliff. "If you're there, I've come to say we forgive them. We forgive the wrong they did you, Black McLean. I've to go away from Scotland and my heart is breaking with it and I have pain in my breast enough to do penance for what they did to you, for two hundred years. My life is done, because I must go, for I'd have liked well to live in Old Jethart till I was an old, old woman. Is that enough pain to satisfy you, McLean, so that you'll lift your harm from those that wronged you? If it's not enough, there's no more I can do."

Auld Rob thought that something frightful would happen. He was staring up at the air beside where I stood, as if he looked for a sign, and then the moon went behind a wisp of muslin and an owl screeched. The sea murmured restlessly far below us and when I looked down, I could see the foam white against the void of the rocks, as the moon came out again.

I could feel no presence of any spirit . . . only a blackness within myself and a numbness and an emptiness . . . desolate.

"I forgive them," I shouted. "Do you hear me? I forgive them."

"For God's sake, hinny. Come awa' frae the cliff edge. 'Twill go oot beneath ye."

"Do you think I care?"

"Come awa' hame, lassie," he said in a shaking voice. "Ye'd not know whit was listening to ye."

He lifted me from the ground and put me on the saddle and he grabbed the bridle and stumbled away up the slope from the cliff.

"They were a' there," he muttered half to himself and I thought that his mind was gone at last. "Every yin o' them. Did ye no' see them, lassie? Black McLean on his white horse and his bonnie bride in front o' him and the Sutherlands with their swords in their scabbards all but ain, and the moon glinting on his blade and his white teeth laughing in his dark face, at the thought of what he'd dae to McLean."

"Don't talk like a daftie, Rob. There was nobody there. It was a fool's errand."

"The McLean's white horse was by yer side," he muttered in terror. "If ye had stretched oot yer hand, ye'd have laid it on the bridle and the bride was smiling doon at ye, for she loved the courage in yer hairt for whit ye did."

I wondered if Rob had been at the whisky bottle to get courage himself and thought it very likely. He was stumbling along the uneven ground as fast as he could go, in a manner very unlike the steady pace he had kept up on the way out.

"I'm sorry I came," I told him and shivered with the cold. "I don't believe in the thing at all and I was a fool to listen to you."

"Naething but guid will cam' frae this nicht's work," he said and hurried along the grass of the hill, that looked across at the other hill, where Old Jethart stood. He stopped the mare suddenly and looked up at me.

"Ye'r a bonnie brave lassie," he said. "I've a mind tae tell ye the rest o' it."

"Oh, Rob!" I exclaimed in despair. "Let's get on home. Maggie will be worried where we are. I know you told her we were going to sort the harness, but it wouldn't take us all this time. She'll come looking for me and find I'm not in the stables and then she'll be angry."

He looked across at the slates of Old Jethart shining in the moonlight.

"It's a blessed place," he sighed and took no notice of what I had said. "There's not a pairson, who sleeps beneath yon roof, that does na feel the enchantment, that's all around it."

"Please take me home, Rob," I begged him.

"'Tis said by some that the spell will be broke' after two hundred years," he said almost to himself. "'Tis said that the one that does it will be a pairson o' great beauty, with a skin as white as milk and eyes as green as the seas round Scarba, her hair dark as the nicht . . . her hairt, as a lion's hairt. They say she'll hae come here greetin' wi' her hairt breakin' to leave the place she loves and that she will serve lang years in a foreign land. They say that while she's gane, the old hoose will mourn her and all the land aboot it will lie fallow, because she's greetin' and alane. The doors will stand open and the daws will build their nests in the tall chimneys, and nettles and thistles will flood the pastures. There'll be a spell on the place, so that a stranger coming within the hoose will lie in his grave 'fore the same season will return the next year, and that is hoo it will be for lang years o' mourning."

Auld Rob was looking up at the wisps of cloud speeding across the sky with the rising wind and at the dark curtain that crept up and crept up from the sea and he looked a strange figure there in the moonlight with the kilt all grey and the glory of the tam o' shanter hidden by the night.

"Then, one day, the dark McLean will come back to Old Jethart," he said, and his voice lifted in triumph. "She'll come ridin' doon the road from Innish, like a queen. The auld hoose will sigh wi' gladness at the sight o' her and the trees bow down their leafy branches at her feet. Her true love will ride by her side and as dark as hersel' and she will walk up the steps to the door and go intae the hoose wi' her man at her side and generations of her bluid will stay in that place in great peace."

I could not understand half he meant to say. The black cloud would cover the moon at any moment and the night would be dark and cold.

"Let's go home," I shivered, not far from tears.

He seemed to come awake again, as if he had been in a trance and I was afraid of him suddenly and knew that it had been foolish to come out on such an errand with such a man. He sighed and started to lead the mare on down the hill and we spoke no more till we came safely into the yard again. I slid down to stand on the cobbles at his side and I looked into his face.

"You're trying to tell me that one day I'll come back here," I said. "You've said a lot of nonsense about a beautiful woman, but you are trying to pretend it is I, and that's all nonsense, the same as it was nonsense about seeing the people out at the cliff. It's kind of you to try to comfort me, but you made it all up from start to finish."

"I made naething up, Mistress McLean," he told me. "Ye think I'm an auld daftie and mabbe I am. But I ken in my hairt the nicht, that as sure as ye stand there before me, that one day, ye'll come riding through yon white gate wi' your man at yer side. Ye were born to restore the old hoose, ye were meant for it, the moment ye were born and ye canna escape yer fate. Why did yer mither run off down the road wi' a McLean, and her head ower heels in love wi' Mister David? She could na help hersel'. It was written in her fate. Ye'll live in this hoose again and it fu' o' happiness, but I'll no' be here to see it. That's why it was shown me the noo. Come oot here one day, when yer first bairn is in his cradle. Stand where ye stand noo. Look back at the lighted windows o' yer hoose and hear yer mon inside, laughing at the joy in his hairt at the sight o' his bairn, and then say that Auld Rob was daft. Mebbe ye'll hear me laughing at yer elbow, but I doot ye will."

I looked at him and I did not know what to make of all he said. My heart was sore at the thought of the next morning and all the time, the fear that Hamish was ill and alone, nagged at my mind.

"I'll say goodbye now, Rob. I'll not get a chance to see you in the morning. Look after Hamish for me. Tell him to try to get to see me, when he's better. Tell him that they wouldn't let me go to him. Thank you for what you tried to do for me. I'd like it fine if it came true, but I've small hopes of it."

He gave a deep sigh.

"Ye think it's a fairy tale, lassie," he said. "But the time will come, when ye're in a foreign land and yer hairt is as sad as it is the nicht. Think o' the headland yonder, for I swear to ye, before God, that I saw the black McLean on his white steed as plain as I see ye noo afore me. The moon was winking in the topazes and amethysts of his horse's heidband. If ye think it's a lie, think o' the gems in the horse's bridle. Any of the folk in these pairts will tell ye the same . . . that McLean aye rade a white horse wi' jewels on its heid. I've heard it a hundred times 'fore tonight and I never kenn't what it meant, for how could a horse hae gems on his heid. I saw it wi' my een, that the gems were on the heidband. McLean was oot on yon leap tonight, after two hundred years and whit would bring him back to Old Jethart, but to see the lassie, brave enough to meet him face to face."

I walked away from him up the yard to the house and my heart was heavy. I went into the kitchen and said goodnight to Maggie and May and then I got into bed and thought of what old Rob had said, but there was not the slightest hope in my mind, what he forecast, would ever come about. I was more certain of it than ever, when I sat beside Miss Burns in her Ford Prefect the next morning and went out through the white gate for the last time. I told her that we must shut the gate after us. Otherwise the cattle and the sheep would stray.

She looked sideways at me and said that she had thought that the stock had all been driven off, but she let me get out to shut the white gate for the last time and I climbed back into the car beside her and as she drove off down the narrow road, the slow tears welled out of my eyes and rolled down my cheeks and splashed on my hands, which I clenched in my lap.

"Maggie told me that you're fretting about not being kept in Scotland," Miss Burns said, not noticing my tears, for I stared hard out of the window and kept my head turned away from her.

"I'd rather stay near here," I said.

"It's all a wee bit difficult," she frowned, "Mountain View" is closing down in a week or two, and I daresay our children will go to Glasgow or Inverness till the new Home is ready. There wouldn't be much advantage in being so far away, would there? You'd be better in your own town in the South, I'm sure."

Her words were dirks, driven under my ribs. In Scotland, I would be near Hamish, who was better, or so Miss Burns said.

"I'd rather stay in Scotland," I said in a muffled voice and she turned to look at me.

"Have you no hanky, Belinda?" she asked me in an artificially friendly voice, and leaned over into the back of the car to pass me a box of tissues. I blew my nose and tried to pull myself together. My whole mind was spinning around in a turmoil of Garry-monkey thoughts, I thought and then I saw that I had forgotten him.

"Garry-monkey!" I cried, "I've forgotten Garry-monkey. Oh, please stop the car. Please turn back for him. He's my oldest friend. I left him on the hall table, so that I shouldn't forget him and he must still be there."

"I'm afraid I haven't the key to the house," she smiled. "Maggie and May will be on the train by now and there's no way of getting in. Besides, aren't you a big lassie to be worrying about a toy monkey?"

She laughed at my troubled face.

"Surely you're past teddybears and dolls and toy monkeys by now?" she teased me.

"He's my mascot," I cried, clasping my hands together. "Oh, please go back for him. He's Garry-monkey. I've had him all my life."

"Don't upset yourself about it," she told me. "We'll write and have him sent on, if you're so set on him. Don't start to greet over a stuffed monkey. He hasn't brought you much luck either, lassie. You might do better to let him lie, where he is. There's plenty of other toys at Mountain View and a pony to ride and everything. I'd forget Garry-monkey if I were you."

I asked them at the Home, as soon as I arrived and the Matron promised to write to the Auctioneers but he still hadn't arrived the next week, when Miss Burns came to fetch me to go to England. I boarded the Royal Scot in Edinburgh and I shared a sleeper with Miss Burns and two strange women and I lay in the top bunk, as the train rushed me farther and farther away from Old Jethart. I had such despair in my heart, as I had never known before. I knew I was bound for the Oaklands Childrens' Home in the Harlton Road in the town I had come from . . . a place I had hoped never to see again in all my life. I thought of the journey north over these same rails with Cousin David five years before, turned my face into the pillow and to muffle the sobs, that tore my chest to bits. I went asleep at last and woke to the rattling of milk churns and I saw that Miss Burns was up and dressed and was washing her false teeth at the basin in the corner and putting them back in her mouth. My eyes burned from my tears and my face was white and miserable, when I looked at it in the mirror.

"When you're fifteen, you'll leave Oaklands and get a job," Miss Burns told me cheerfully in the taxi on the way to the Home. "You'll be in care for three years till you're eighteen years of age and then you can please yourself. We'll get work for you in Scotland and you can come back to the Highlands again. Don't fret, hinny."

I carried my case from the taxi to the door of the Home. I knew it well. It was a modern yellow building like a pile of baby's bricks all thrown higgledy-piggledy down in a grassy field. It had a bright yellow door and Miss Burns pressed the bell and I heard it ring somewhere inside the house and for a long time, nothing happened and then there were steps coming along the hall and the door opened. It was a fattish woman in a pink nylon overall and she was square and short and her hair looked greasy and grey. She smiled at us and held out her hand to shake Miss Burns's hand and then she turned to me.

"You'll be Belinda," she said. "You'll be tired after your long trip. Come into my office and we'll see about a cup of tea."

We went into the hall and there was a small boy, standing in the corner with his face to the wall. He was crying to himself in a very miserable way.

"That's Jimmy McDonald," the woman said sharply and I

thought that her voice had a spiteful edge to it, although she was smiling still. "He went into the pantry and put his fingers into the marmalade jar and he's to stand there, till he learns he's not to do it again. Aren't you, Jimmy?"

Jimmy's crying got a shade louder and he wiped his nose on his cuff. The woman gave him a prod in the back as she passed and she pretended it was in fun and laughed at it, but there was spite in it too.

"It won't be the corner next time, will it, Jimmy?" she asked him. "It will be the cane across your tail end."

I thought that she relished the idea of beating the child in some queer dark way and I did not like her one bit, but she turned to us, all sugar and gush and made us sit down by the gas fire and rang for tea for us. I wanted quite badly to go to the lavatory and I asked her if I might be excused and she took me through a pair of bright red swing doors and pointed down a long wide passage to a green door at the far end. I walked along the polished floor and wondered what would happen if I ran away. I got sick in the lavatory and then I turned on the cold tap and dashed the water into my face. After a while, I went back down the passage to the office door and Jimmy looked round at me, with despair in his eyes. I smiled at him and told him not to cry. There was nothing to cry about, I said. Nobody minded standing in the corner.

"She twisted my ear," he sniffled. "Old Beastly twisted my ear off."

I tapped at the door and went in and I saw that my papers were out on the desk. There was a long typed list, that the woman had started to fill in. I had had a similar one at Mountain View, but this was longer, or so I thought. I glanced down at my name and age all written in small tidy block letters.

"Date of admission . . . today," said the woman to herself and turned to tell me to help myself to a cup of tea and a biscuit. The tea was in a strange glass cup and I picked it up and drank a sip of it and my eye ran down the list of garments.

Vests, knickers, suspender belts, brassieres, underskirts, dresses, blouses, skirts, shorts, gym slip, cardigans, shoes, sandals, slippers, stockings, pyjamas, hats, overcoats, rain coats, gloves, handkerchiefs, towels, flannel, toothbrush, comb, brush (hair), jumpers, suitcase, Bible, Cash, other items.

"You know that this is your new Matron, Mrs. Greastly," Miss Burns told me and I smiled and said I did, although it was a lie. They were sorting my clothes out on a table and Mrs. Greastly was ticking in the numbers opposite the item on the list.

"I forgot to bring my toy monkey from Old Jethart," I said, looking up into the woman's pasty face. "I've had him a long time and I wouldn't like to lose him. Do you think I might write to the people about him?"

Miss Burns turned her head to stare at me through her glasses.

"I'm afraid it would be a waste of time, Belinda. We've been into that in Mountain View and they've looked and he's just not there. I'm afraid he's away to the Auction Room with all the other stuff and anyhow you're too big to greet after a stuffed monkey now."

Mrs. Greastly was sorting my things.

"Vests," she muttered to herself. "Knickers. Suspender belts... two. One on you, I suppose?"

She raised her heavy eyebrows at me and I said "yes".

She frowned.

"You say 'Yes, Mrs. Greastly,' she told me and turned back to her list. "Bodices, three. Underskirt, nil. Dresses..."

She picked up a pair of breeches.

"These will be no good to you here," she said and gave them to Miss Burns. "Better let them go back to Mountain View. I believe you've got a pony there. We don't run to such grandeur in Oaklands, I'm afraid."

There was the same little cutting, sneering edge to her voice.

"Besides, they stink," she said and wrinkled her nose. "Your suitcase smells like the stables. We'll have to have you wash it out in disinfectant, Belinda."

"How much money has she got?" she asked Miss Burns when she came near the end of the list, picking up my purse from the table.

"Have you any in your pockets?"

She did not wait for an answer, but came over and put her hand in each of my pockets and then opened my coat and looked in my dress pockets. She counted it out on her desk.

"Thirty-three and a half new pence."

I felt like a prisoner, as indeed I suppose I was. I began to feel panic rise in me like the tide.

"One bible, one prayer-book, one hymnal," she said, and picked up the white book of poems. It opened at their poem, as it always did and she glanced down at it.

"How do I love thee? Let me count the ways . . ." she read out in a hard voice, devoid of any feeling or tenderness whatever. She raised the dark brows at Miss Burns, who had gone to sit beside the fire again, and the sunlight made her glasses flash as she turned to look at me.

"Did you do this at school?" she asked me and I said "Yes, Mrs. Greastly," It was the easiest thing to say. How could I ever begin to tell her what the book meant to me? She threw it carelessly down on top of the Bible and I picked it up and held it tightly against my chest.

She came over and put a hand on my hair. Slowly and with method, she divided it and went carefully all over my scalp.

"She's clean," said Miss Burns from her chair by the fire. "You can save yourself the time of doing that. I told you the sort of home she came from. The laird was her Guardian. She's not one to have creepie-crawlies in her head."

"Better safe than sorry," the matron replied shortly. "I don't want to have to write up to Mountain View and tell them they've sent me a dirty head, so I'd better look, hadn't I?"

Miss Burns sniffed and I thought that she liked Mrs. Greastly no better than I did, but she said nothing.

"Have you got her Medical Card?" the Matron asked her.

"She had a private doctor in the Highlands, but here's her old card. I expect she's still on this man's list in the town here. Dove's his name."

Miss Burns got up and opened her handbag, which was on the desk. She took out several cards and put them down one by one.

"Medical Card," she said. "Baptism Card, Birth Certificate, National Savings Book, but there's nothing in it, poor bairn. She's spent up."

Mrs. Greastly looked at each of them in turn and took out another form from her desk.

"McLean. Belinda Mary Stuart! There's a mouthful for you. I wish parents would think of the poor devils, who have to fill in forms, when they choose their children's names . . . Old Jethart, Innish, Argyll, Scotland. Religion, Church of England."

"Has she been vaccinated and inoculated?" she asked Miss Burns and Miss Burns nodded her head.

Mrs. Greastly lowered her voice to a pitch, which she may have thought was not audible to me, as she went on "Father dead. Mother dead. Other children in the family. Nil. Relations. Nil. Goodness gracious me! What a lot of blanks! . . . anybody else interested?"

She turned to Miss Burns.

"Anybody else interested?" she said aloud.

Miss Burns looked uncomfortable and shook her head.

"The family servants, perhaps. Maggie and May McCullough."

She thought for a moment.

"The one most concerned would be her guardian's cousin, Hamish Sutherland. He's a very distant relative too, I think, but not enough to count. If he gets better, there's no doubt he'd be interested to know how she was doing, but he's in the West Highland Hospital in Oban at the moment, and he's got double pneumonia."

I had not been told that and Miss Burns had not intended it to slip out either. It was the final straw, which broke what self-control, I had left.

"If he's badly ill, I want to go to him," I cried. "He'll have nobody, if I don't go. Oh, please take me back to Scotland and let me see him."

I grabbed Miss Burns by the hands, but she shook her head at me and told me to be a good girl.

I knelt down at her feet on the ground and wept into the front of her blue gaberdine coat.

"Don't leave me alone, Miss Burns," I wept. "Please take me back to the other home. I don't like it here. Please don't go away and leave me here."

I burst out into a flood of weeping, all my pride gone and Miss Burns stooped down and lifted me to my feet.

"Dinna kneel tae me, lassie," she said, her voice all gone to her native Scots, in her distress.

"Rise up, noo, there's ma guid hinny and stop that greetin' for 'twill dae ye no guid. Ye know I'd not leave ye here, if I'd my say. We'd hae liked weil for ye to stay but it's no tae be. Dinna make it worse for yoursel'."

I wept louder and my voice broke in hysteria. I sobbed like a little girl and the Matron came over and screamed at me to stop the noise at once.

I slipped through Miss Burns's hands and went on my knees again in supplication to her.

"I don't want to stay here," I cried to Miss Burns. "I want to go back to Old Jethart. I will never be happy here. It's a horrid place and it's too far away. If you leave me here, I'll run away and I'll follow you home like a dog . . . and if you drive me away, and I'm brought here again, I'll only run away again. I'll run away, I tell you. I'll run away. I'll run away, I tell . . ."

Mrs. Greastly's open hand took me across the cheek with a slap, that rattled the teeth in my head. She cut off my words, as if she had turned them off at a tap. She could have stopped then, but she did not stop. She lifted her other hand and struck me across the other cheek for good measure and her eyes were happy, because she was hitting me.

She took me by the shoulder and looked down into my eyes.

"You're to go to your room now and you're to change into your gym slip and white blouse. Then you'll come straight downstairs and you'll apologise to me. Miss Burns will be gone by then, so you'd better say goodbye to her now."

I took Miss Burns's hand and said "Goodbye, Miss Burns. Thank you for being so kind to me."

She put her arms about me and hugged me tightly and then she stooped down and kissed me. I knew she was wondering if it was worth making a fuss with Mrs. Greastly about the scene. There were strict rules about beating, one of the children at Mountain View had told me.

"There's nothing so good for hysteria as a sharp slap on the cheek," Mrs. Greastly remarked to her, with a smile, and at that, Miss Burns decided that it was not worth saying anything about it.

"Come into the dining room now and have a proper breakfast," Mrs. Greastly went on. "Belinda will have hers, when she comes down and we make friends again."

She smiled at me and put her arm about my shoulders to lead me to the door and the last I ever saw of Miss Burns was her rueful worried face as she watched me go.

That was how I was handed over to "the care and protection" of Mrs. Greastly and I was to remain under it for the next year or so. Looking back on it now, there is no doubt that she was unbalanced mentally. She was like a rotten apple, that turns a whole barrel of sound apples rotten too. She affected the Home, from the staff to the youngest child, by her cruelty. We were shared out between five house mothers. There were fifty of us all told. I had the luck to be allotted to Auntie Jill, who was a fair, sturdy girl with a spotty face and very blue eyes. She had a rough, kind cheerfulness with us and I do not know how I could have got through the next year without her.

The doctor was the first one who really helped me and I went along to see him in the Medical Room the first time he visited the Home after my arrival. Auntie Jill told me that I was wanted in the Medical Room for my examination and I looked at her in dismay.

"What will they do with me?" I asked her.

"Dr. Evans is a terrible man," she laughed. "He likes little girls stuffed with chestnuts for his dinner. He'll truss you up and put you in the oven and baste your chest with lard and then he'll sit down and eat you . . . slice by slice."

She laughed and came over to pull me towards the door by the plait.

"What do you think he'll do to you?" she cried and smacked my bottom. "He'll just give you the once-over, you daft ha'porth . . . look at your teeth and see if you want false ones or a wig or a wooden leg and if you do, he'll write a prescription for you."

She saw I was still worried about it and put her arm round my shoulders.

"He'll look in your mouth and in your ears. It's not bad. None of the children mind it. He'll tap you on the chest and the back and listen to you . . . the usual old stuff . . . nothing to worry over."

There was a small dismal queue outside the Medical Room,

when I arrived and I stood at the back and listened to Mrs. Greastly's harsh voice through the door. I saw Jimmy McDonald waiting to go first and he was holding his ear in his grubby hand. He looked up into my face.

"It was Old Beastly, wot done it," he whimpered and wiped his nose on his cuff.

I found the solution to my sorrow that day and it was very simple. It was to stop being selfish to stop striving to alter my own state and try to help others. Jimmy McDonald came up to me that day and put his face against my waist and his arms about me.

"Tell me a story," he sniffed.

We moved up the passage a little way and I squatted down with Jimmy's arms about my neck.

"I'll tell you a story about a wonderful place I knew once," I said, and sixteen eyes never left my face. "It was a place in Scotland, high up in the biggest mountains you could ever imagine. They were so big that the snow lay on their heads all the winter and sometimes the clouds came down to cover them."

"Wot was it called?" asked Jimmy.

"It was called Old Jethart and it was a lovely place, with a grey house that stood on a hill, and a river that ran in the glen. There was a white gate, with a very special catch on it, so that you did not have to get off your horse, as you rode in..."

I lost my audience one by one, as the doctor called them in.

"There were six brothers, who lived in this house a long, long time ago and they had a very beautiful sister, who fell in love with a prince, that they hated. He came to the house one night on a white horse, with a jewelled headband and he knocked at the door. The moon was out and the precious stones glittered and winked in the light from it, and then the sister came out and her eyes were even brighter than the jewels in the headband..."

"Belinda McLean."

I went into the room and stood before the desk and the old man looked at me kindly.

"Belinda Mary Stuart McLean." he said. "That's a fine Scots name for a bonnie lassie."

I thought for a moment he was a Scot and my heart lifted, but he was only joking with me by putting on the accent.

"She's an English girl," put in Mrs. Greastly, who sat by his side. "She was born in the town, not far from here."

"I know. I know," he said irritably. "I have that all here. She's still a bonnie wee lassie and she's come from Innish in Argyll and that's where I go every year in May and October to shoot and fish ... at least not to Innish, but to a place not twenty miles away. I go two months a year and I wish I went for twelve, so you know what I think of Innish, Argyll, my dear."

He smiled at me.

He looked at my papers and muttered to himself. "Nobody interested in her except two old servants and a distant cousin indeed. I'm interested in her for one and there are plenty of others too, if they practise what they preach. Come round and stand by me here, where I can see you properly, for I daresay my eyes aren't so sharp as yours."

I went round the desk and he held me tightly against his warm side and I smelt the smell of his shaving soap and his tobacco, so that I remembered Cousin David and felt the old stab in my chest again, as I did a hundred times a day.

"I'm your friend," he started off. "Do you believe me?"

I nodded my head and Mrs. Greastly said "Say, yes, thank you, Doctor."

I said it at once and he looked at her irritably, and then turned back to talk to me.

"I've got to see if you are a strong girl and find out if there is any little thing wrong, which I could put right. It's nothing unpleasant or frightening and I'm sure your own doctor has examined you many times and I know by the look of you that you're a good patient..."

"Do you like it here?" he shot out at me, when he had finished with me, and I looked over at Mrs. Greastly quickly and then back at him and said "Yes, thank you, Doctor."

He caught the look too and knew what it meant.

"Before you go, I'll say one thing to you," he said. "*Tempora mutantur*,' It is Latin and it was said a very long time ago. It means that times change. Nothing can go on for ever, can it Belinda?"

I knew the quotation, for Hamish had taught it to me. I said it all to him.

"*Tempora mutantur, et nos mutamur in illis*." I said with a smile, "It's the last bit I'm afraid of, sir."

He sat up in his chair, as if a golden guinea had fallen out of my mouth.

"Where did you learn that?" he asked, and I told him all about Hamish and the table by the fire in the sitting room. I told him how Cousin David used to listen to our lessons and how he used to wink at me behind Hamish's back and eventually I told him of the sally switch and he said "I should think so too." I was quite carried away with the happy memory of it all and I forgot where I was and was back in Old Jethart again. I was recalled by Mrs. Greastly's voice.

"Her I.Q. is high, Doctor," she said.

The doctor looked at me and laughed.

"It may not be high enough for you to know what it means, Belinda Mary Stuart, but it means that you're no fool. Would you like to go to the High School, instead of going out to work, when you're fifteen?"

I nodded my head. I could not even say thank you and

Mrs. Greastly glared at me, for my bad manners.

"I don't think there would be any chance of a place for her at her present age," she declared. "They go up there, if they pass the eleven plus."

He put up a hand to stroke my hair and asked me how far I had got in Latin and how far in French and what else Hamish had taught me and at last, he sat back in his chair and stuck his hands into the pocket of his white coat.

"Mr. James, the Education Officer is a patient of mine. I might add, a grateful patient," he said. "He is foolish enough to think that it was I, and not the Almighty, who saved the life of his only child on the night of his birth. He might be able to get something done. They're usually willing to sever red tape in exceptional circumstances. *'Tempora mutantur'* indeed, *'et nos in illis.'* It would be a pity to set the diamond in tin, instead of in precious metal. Eh, Mrs. Greastly?"

She looked at me and I could see the dislike in her eyes.

"I'm sure I'd be delighted if we could help Belinda in any way, Doctor. We are all very fond of her in Oaklands. She's a quiet girl and she's a great help with the babies. I don't know when we've had such a nice child. Once she settles down here and gets all this Scotch nonsense out of her head, we'll get on fine, I'm sure."

She told me I could go back to the play room shortly after that and no more was said about the High School. I thought it very unlikely that I would hear any more about it and then one day, Mr. James, the Education Officer, called and spoke to me for a long time in the Office, with Mrs. Greastly listening to every word and making it hard for me to remember anything at all of what I had learnt from Hamish. He went off eventually and no more was said, till Auntie Jill came into the play room one day and told me to put on my hat and coat.

"We're off to town to fit you out for the High School, Miss McLean. I believe you're to attend there and learn Latin and

French and Tripe and onions and I don't know what. My word! Ain't we all gone posh? I hope that they won't make you feel too high and mighty to talk to your old Auntie Jill in a month or so. Come on now! Don't stand there gawking at me, with your mouth open. We must catch the next bus to town or it won't be Latin, Mrs. G. will be talking to me. Parlez-vous, Mam'zelle. Oui! Oui! And that doesn't mean that you're to do it in your trousers, while I'm gone, Jimmy McDonald."

I ran to her and put my arms about her and hugged her and she swung me round and round and round till we were both dizzy.

"Oh, Auntie Jill! I said. "Oh, Auntie Jill!"

"Come on, Belinda McLean! I'll give you Auntie Jill. You run and get your things on and off we'll go, before the Education Officer, the Lord High James changes his mind and sends you off to Holloway Jail."

She teased me about being posh, but it was all in good part, Mrs. Greastly did it too, but she was bitter and sneering with it. It may be my imagination, but I do not think it was. She called me "Miss Toffee Nose." and "Miss Haughty Drawers" but she meant to hurt me. Auntie Jill asked me what I had done to Old Beastly. "She's got her knife into you, Belinda," she told me.

I started at the High School on the first day of term and set off on the bus in my school hat and my blue gaberdine raincoat and I was pleased that I was going to get a chance to prove myself. I was sensible enough to realise that with a High School education behind me, I would get a far better job, than if I left school at fifteen, and I had plans for making enough money one day, to buy back Old Jethart.

I was very happy at school. I think the Mistresses singled me out for special kindness, knowing that I came from Oaklands. I used to turn towards the Harlton Road every evening, with a sinking of the heart, leaving the bright friendly atmosphere of the school and knowing that Mrs. Greastly was lying, like a snake under a stone, waiting for a chance to strike out at me. I think that she did her best to make the other children join with her in jeering at my "snob education", as she called it, and if she had succeeeded, I should have been very poor indeed, but I was making a name for myself in the home, as a person to whom one could run for a little sympathy and help, and my stories were already in great demand. It was a strange sort of life compared to that of Old Jethart. I got up at half past six and helped Auntie Jill get the little ones washed and dressed and then we went down to breakfast and served theirs and had our own too. I got on a bus outside the gates at eight fifteen and made my way to school, with my books in a satchel. At five o'clock, I was back again to help get the children fed and to bed and then I settled down in the quiet room to try to master my homework.

I had asked Mrs. Greastly to let me write to Hamish and wrote to him fairly regularly. Mrs. Greastly did not know it, but Auntie Jill had seen the state I was in, that first day and had earned my undying love, by sneaking out to a call box and ringing the hospital for news of him. She found out that he had developed pneumonia the day after Cousin David's accident and had got some complications, which made him very ill for a few weeks. I know now that it was a lung abscess and that he was not expected to live for many weeks and they had thought it merciful to tell me nothing about it. I got his first letter when I had been a month in the home and I took it up to the room I shared with four of the smaller children. I sat on the bed and looked at his familiar writing and thought of the way he had written on my copy books in Old Jethart.

"My dearest Lindy, I am so glad to hear that you are settled down in the new Home. It is great news about the possibility of attending High School and I hope that something will come of it. I have been lying here for a long time, trying to make plans for both of us and I have been more worried about you having to quit school at fifteen, than I have about anything else. I have but to close my eyes and I am back in the sitting room with you beside me, sitting at the table, your plaits down your shoulders, trying not to yawn at the mystery of Latin verse and trying to catch Cousin David's eye, behind my back, as he sits pretending to read a book. '*Eheu fugaces*!' and I hope you remember what that means, you young dunderhead! I have plans to work as Steward on Lord Clochan's estate and will start as soon as I am out of hospital, which should not be long now. I will come down to see you at the first opportunity. Be sure of that and '*Nil desperandum*'. If you had attended to my lessons more at the time, you would know what that means now. As to definite dates, Lord Clochan always goes to London for the Chelsea Flower Show in May. With any luck, he will take me and I will get to see you again. I have a scheme to make enough money to put down a deposit on Old Jethart and eventually buy it back. Anybody I have discussed it with, thinks I'm daft. The only one who agrees with me that it is a brilliant plan is your old enemy, Jock McGregor, whose nose you bled your first day at Innish School. I hope that you agree with him too, but you must wait till I see you and I will tell you all about it. In the meantime, don't lose your hope of being back one day in Old Jethart. I'll never rest till I see that dream come true. With all my love. Hamish."

He came to see me in May. He walked in quite unexpectedly one Tuesday night, looking very strange and Scots in his tweed jacket and swinging kilt. He spoke to Mrs. Greastly for five minutes, and then I was sent along to the reception room to see him. I ran along the polished corridor and threw open the yellow door of the room. He was standing at the far end with his back to the mantelpiece, over which hung the picture of the Raphael Madonna. I went down the thick Indian carpet like a frightened rabbit and flung myself into his arms and had a job not to burst into tears and ask him to take me home with him and not go away and leave me in this awful place. I hugged him so hard with my arms tightly round his neck, that I must have been in danger of choking him, but he did not complain. I buried my face against his shoulder and blinked back my tears before he saw them and his mouth came down to rest on the top of my head.

"Oh, Hamish!" I whispered. "It's so good to see you. You don't know what it's like to be able to hug you again. It's been so long, Hamish. It's been like fifty million years."

He rested his chin against my head, and still held me tightly, and when he thought I had got rid of the tears, he held me away from him and looked me up and down. He let me go suddenly and walked across to the window.

"You've got awfu' small," he said and said nothing else for a long time. He turned round at last and came back and seized me by the shoulders quite fiercely.

"I'll get you out of this damned place, if it's the last thing I do. It's all my fault you happen to be here, but I'll get you free of it. I swear before God, I'll see you back in Old Jethart again, where you long to be, or may I rot in hell."

"Tell me about the plans, Hamish," I begged him. "You told me in your letters, that you had two and I must choose."

He sat me down on a chair and walked up and down the room for a bit and then he came to stand before me.

"Perhaps it had better be the first one," he said dourly. "It'd get you out of here far quicker than the one I had set my heart on."

"What is it?" I asked him. "I'd like it to be soon . . . very soon, if you could think of a way."

"I could take me a wife," he said, flatly. "It doesn't matter who, but I'd pick a decent girl, who'd be good to you and then I'd adopt you as my daughter."

I had to smile at his miserable face, for it was quite easy to see he had no liking for it.

"I don't think it would work. It would be a terrible thing if you were to be tied to a decent woman . . . you, who only liked giggling blond girls."

"You haven't forgotten how to smile then?" he said with a ghost of a grin. "I thought maybe you had."

"You'd better tell me the other way. I can wait a bit. It won't seem long, if we have something to hope for."

"There's a car ferry to be started across the loch at Clochan," he told me. "It's not far from the old place. We used to swim there. Do you remember?"

I nodded my head and remembered it far too well.

" 'Twill save twenty miles of road and it's the main way to the glen. All the trippers will be using it. I have a mind to build two huts . . . one on the north side and one on the south. I have the money for it and for two petrol pumps too. I'll have two wee huts, very simple places and I'll sell cigarettes and sweeties and postcards and soft drinks. I'll keep one of them myself and put Jock McGregor in the other. We'll catch the tourists coming both ways."

"That's wonderful!" I cried and hugged him in my arms again and felt the rough tweed against my face. "That's wonderful Hamish! It couldn't fail."

"You're the only one, who thinks so," he said. "Only for myself and Jock."

He held me away from him and looked down into my eyes again.

" 'Twill take a fair while," he warned me. "I've been counting it up. Three years at best and perhaps four, five, six. I'd buy Old Jethart back in the end of it and then I promise you, 'twill be yours too, as well as mine."

He let me go and walked away to the window and looked out into the darkness of the grounds.

"Nobody has bought it yet," he said. "They're a superstitious lot up there. They say there's bad luck on it, for a stranger to buy it. They say that the bank should not have turned us out. There's none will touch it and 'twill go for a song in a few years . . . say three or four."

"But I'll be eighteen by then," I said in dismay. "It wouldn't be proper for me to go to live with you in the house by our two selves. I'll be a woman grown."

He stood and looked at me and smiled a little. I was wearing my navy gym slip and it was as short as a skating skirt. I had on a white blouse and the red and white High School tie and my hair was divided in the centre and hung in plaits on my shoulders. How could he have romantic thoughts about me? How could he know that I was a woman already and loved him very much? How could he know what his answer did to my heart?

"I'll find me a wife by then. There's plenty of time. I'll get a bonnie wee fair lassie with blue eyes, who will laugh all day long and fill the house wi' bairns, and you can come to Old Jethart to mind them for us, so that I can spend the whole day, kissing the porker under the mistletoe, without the bairns under our feet."

He laughed a long time and looked as happy as he had ever been and I wondered if it was the thought of the fair lassie and was consumed with jealousy. He bent down and kissed my cheek.

"I love you, Belinda Mary Stuart. I think you're the lassie to mind my bairns for me all right and no mistake."

He was serious suddenly.

"Can you wait three years . . . perhaps four, for me? Can you put up with that she-devil I saw when I came in? Don't let them break you, my bonnie black corbie. When it gets too bad, close your eyes and come to Old Jethart to me, for it's there I'll be every minute of every day in my heart. Come back through the white gate and we'll ride the avenue, side by side, like the old times, loose the horses in the stables and go in to the fire and your hand in mine."

He saw the tears on my cheeks, for I could no more stop their flowing than I could turn back the tide at the bottom of the cliff, or lift the moon down out of the sky.

"It won't be long, my beautiful dark hinny. Wait for me, my dearie. If I don't come south, it's not that my heart isn't aching for the sight of you. Can you bear the waiting, my wee dove?"

"It won't be long, Dominie," I lied to him and then I stood and watched the swing of his kilt, as he went away. I watched through the window, but it was too dark to see beyond the light out at the gate. He turned there and lifted his hand in farewell and I felt the loneliness come creeping into my breast again. I went back down the corridor very slowly and sat with my lesson books before me till it was time to go to bed. The loneliness was an emptiness in my chest till I closed my eyes and imagined how it was when I came in on Lady Judy through the white gate. The lambs would be white on the green of the hill, for it was May. The bluebells would be out and the clumps of primroses. The waterfalls would be filling the whole air with their music in this secret world to which I escaped at night time. I dreamt I was back in Old Jethart that night and it was all as it had been, and when I woke, I turned my face into my pillow in bitterness because it was only a dream.

PART FIVE

I took a bottle of milk and two sandwiches to school every day and often Auntie Jill would put a bar of chocolate or an apple as a surprise in my satchel. She always walked, in rain or shine, down the drive as far as the gate with me, saw me off every morning and waved to me as I stood on the platform of the bus.

I had an hour for my lunch in school and I was free to do as I pleased. There was a park nearby and I often went along and sat on a bench to watch the ducks in the lake. It was because of this picnic in the park most days that I came to meet "Old Trad" and it must have been a very lucky day indeed, when I stopped to look into the window of his shop. I had passed it by many times before, but the day after Hamish's visit I saw that he had put out some books on a stand and I looked along the titles to see if there was a nice copy of *Cranford*, which we were reading at school. Of course, there wasn't, but my eye was caught by a flash of yellow and brown in the back of the rather dirty window. I leaned forward to see what it was and my heart nearly leaped into my mouth, for it looked like Garry-monkey, yet I knew it could not be he. It must be a toy monkey, just like him, for he had the same slightly miserable, little-bit-downcast expression on his face. I put my hand into my pocket and took out my money to count it, to see if it could have increased by magic, from the ten new pence for the bus fare home, but of course, it had not. I walked into the shop and my knees felt like feathers for all the support they were giving me. There was a dusty mirror on the back of the wall behind the counter and I saw that my face was as white as a sheet and my eyes as big as saucers, under the brim of the straw-boater, with its red and white ribbon. There was nobody in the shop and I thought it was very poky and low-ceilinged. It smelt very old and dusty and stuffy. There was a curtained doorway, which led to a room at the back and the counter was a showcase of very scratched, dim glass, in which were things of antique interest, such as brooches, rings, gold chains, gold bracelets, old watches, little silver penknives and all manner of other jewellery. I waited for what seemed a very long time and my hands were shaking so much that I put them in my pockets and then I thought that might look rude, so I took them out again. At last, I gave a small apologetic cough, which was more a clearing of the throat than a cough, and I heard a chair scrape against the floor inside the curtain.

Then the curtain was pulled aside by a hand and a man in a peaked cap put his head out and saw that there was a customer, so he came out into the shop and looked down at me and I thought that he was the strangest person I had ever seen. He wore a navy battledress blouse and it was covered on the breast with ribbon medals. There were real medals too, which tinkled together in front of his tunic. He had a black cap, like a seaman might wear, with a shiny peak to it and his hair was white and curled out from under it. His face was almost covered with a white beard, cut into a trim naval point beneath his chin and his eyes were light blue and clear and twinkling.

I looked at him shyly.

"I hope that I didn't take you from your dinner," I said. "I can wait till you're finished, or come back again, if that's better."

He bowed very courteously and put his hands flat down on the glass of the counter, not taking his eyes off mine. There was a strange sad look in his face, that I was at a loss to account for.

"You do not incommode me in the slightest, Madam," he said in a deep rich voice like an actor might have. "What is it your pleasure that I show you?"

I got more awkward than ever. After all, I had no money.

"I'm not a proper customer, really," I stammered. "I . . . I . . . I haven't any money except my bus fare home, so if you were to finish your dinner first, it wouldn't matter at all."

"What item were you interested in?" he asked me, looking at me keenly, as if he wanted to see if I was joking.

"It's the toy monkey in the back of the window, sir," I said hesitantly. "It's an awfully long story really and you might not want to listen to it. It's not terribly interesting."

"My time is at your disposal, Duchess," he said in a grand manner, shooting out his arms to the side, palms upwards.

My hands were shaking so badly that I clasped them behind my back, but my voice trembled and gave me away.

"I had a toy monkey, called Garry," I started. "When Mother died, I took him to Old Jethart with me. My Cousin David came down and took me from the flat. It was two rooms really. Mother and I weren't very rich, but it was lovely with Cousin David in Scotland. Then, when he died, there was no money left and I had to go under care and protection. Maggie and May would have had me, if they could, but they had to go to work and the Scottish people didn't want me, because I belonged here. They brought me to Oaklands Childrens' Home and that's where I am now. The bus fare is to take me back there tonight."

I paused then for want of breath, for it had all come out in a rush and he smiled at me in a very kind way, that made me feel better.

"Have you no father either?" he asked me in a gentle quiet voice, and I shook my head and told him that Father had been dead a long time and I didn't even remember seeing him.

"A child a man might give a king's ransome to possess," he

sighed to nobody in particular. "A waif of the storms and nobody to cherish her!"

He folded his arms on his chest and I went on with my story.

"I had this Garry-monkey," I said. "He was a pessimist. I learnt that in school the other day and I said to myself "That's Garry-monkey all over!" He was always thinking of all the very worst things, that could happen and he was usually right in the end too."

I looked up at him anxiously.

"He didn't really think," I explained. "He was only sawdust. I used to pretend it in a childish way, before I grew up and knew it was silly."

"Perhaps it wasn't silly," he remarked. "That fellow in the window there is always putting thoughts in my head. If I happen to be feeling low or depressed, I pick up my young friend there and he says "Cheer up, Trad!" That's what he says "Things aren't all that bad. There's never a cloud without a silver lining."

"My Garry-monkey would never say a thing like that," I told him with a smile. "Perhaps that isn't he after all. I'd like to look at him all the same, Mr. Trad, because I'd know him by his crew cut, and maybe by his clothes. I left him behind at Old Jethart, because I was sad at leaving and he was lying on the hall table, waiting for me. It was terribly careless, but I was trying not to be a baby and I quite forgot Garry-monkey and they could never find him afterwards. It didn't matter, I suppose, because I was too big for teddy bears and dolls. I was fourteen turned."

"Were you up in Scotland then?" he asked me sharply and looked at me very thoughtfully. "I should think he might be your friend after all. That young man came from a place up north . . . a long way up . . . not far from the sea. What was the name of your place?"

158

"Innish in Argyll," I said anxiously.

He nodded his head and leaned into the window, through a little door he opened in the back of it. He picked the monkey up and gave it to me.

"He might be a little changed," he said, with a sideways look at my face.

I bent my head down over the golliwog and thought that he looked a bit different, although his face was very sad still. I pretended that I wanted to concentrate very hard on him and I laid him on the counter and kept my head down, but a tear fell on his yellow jumper, so I picked him up quickly and took him to the door, as if I wanted to see him in the light, till I got my face right again. He had the same sort of clothes, I saw, but they were not Garry-monkey's clothes. I knew every stitch of every set of garments he possessed.

"His clothes are different," I said doubtfully. "The crew cut looks the same, but the clothes aren't Garry-monkey's."

I came back and laid him down on the counter with a sigh.

"I don't think it's Garry-monkey," I said, another small world in ruins about me.

He looked at me more keenly than ever and went off into the back room for a minute. Then he came back and leaned both hands on the counter.

"If it's the clothes you're worried about, don't take notice of them. He had a different kit on him when he came in and they'd got a bit dirty with the packing. I had them replaced. The moth had got into them too and probably a bit into his hair. I trimmed that up somewhat..."

I asked him if he was sure he had got him from Innish, Argyll, and he took out a ledger, turned his back on me and asked me how it was spelt.

I spelt it out carefully and he gave a snort of triumph.

"Here it is!" he cried. "That chap was in a consignment from Innish. A shop at Oban had it. It was the property of a deceased gentleman called Mister David something, can't read my own writing these days..."

"Sutherland," I whispered, and he snapped the book shut in a small cloud of dust.

"There's no doubt about it. That's your Garry-monkey. Isn't that a wonderful coincidence, my lady?"

I hugged Garry-monkey to my chest and turned round from side to side in a swinging dance of delight. I sang him a short song and I smiled down at him, because I knew that he would be as pleased as I was. Then I remembered that I had no money and my heart turned to lead. I put him down on the counter regretfully, although I still held his hand to comfort myself.

"Would it be a great deal of trouble to you, sir," I asked hesitantly looking up into his face. "If you were to put him aside for me and I'd bring you my pocket money each week till he's paid for? I get twenty new pence every Saturday in Mrs. Greastly's office. I don't know how much you're asking for him, but I'd go on bringing you the money till it was enough. I couldn't get it to you till Monday at lunch time, but I'd have it here every week just after one o'clock, if you'd not mind waiting."

"My very dear young lady!" he exclaimed. "Do not distress yourself. There has been a dreadful error on somebody's part. This young Garry-monkey should never have come into my possession in the first place. I had no right in the world to have exhibited him for sale in my shop window, although strictly speaking, he was not for sale. He just chanced to be in there today to see what was going on in the street. It used to be one of his favourite places at one time... when he came here first."

He took out a large white handkerchief and blew his nose loudly and then replaced the handkerchief in his pocket.

"I expect he was on the look out for you, because he knew it was a mistake that he was left behind on the table. I very much fear that I may have broken the law, you know, dear Countess. Take him quickly before I am apprehended for possessing stolen property. I will never forgive myself that this happened. A thousand apologies, Madam, and it would make me a very happy man, if you would consent to take a dish of tea in my parlour, as a token that you forgive me."

He had pushed Garry into my arms and I hugged the poor monkey, in a way, which must have been very uncomfortable for his sawdust feelings. I went round under a flap in the counter and Mr. Trad sat me down at a table covered with a red velvet cloth with bobbles, gave me a cup of tea presently and some biscuits from a glass barrel with a silver lid.

"I think that Garry-monkey missed you," he mused, sipping his tea. "It's a strange thing, but soft living ruins a man's character. Give me a person, whose life has been fired in the kiln of adversity. It puts a fine temper in the steel, does adversity, my lady. It's the same thing with plants, you know. They put down their roots in the harsh weather."

I sat with Garry clasped to my breast, not making much of what he said.

"Now that gentleman is quite a reformed character," he went on. "You can take it from me. He's an optimist and as you know, of course, that is the very opposite of a pessimist. Do you know that, the other day, I was feeling sad? I started to think that I was a lonely old man, wife and child gone . . . nobody to care a tinker's curse for me . . . no friends left . . . all gone. Garry-monkey looked up at me and he told me that self-pity is the worst sin of all. Do you know what he said? He said "Look at the sunshine and listen to the birds. God's in his heaven, man. Go up to the park and see the flowers. Think of all your blessings! Your wife and Sadie are not lost. Don't ever doubt that there's a God and he keeps them in his tender care for you. You're not poor or destitute. You have a sound roof over your head and food to eat. Come on now, old Trad.

Let's have a smile," I couldn't help smiling at him, my lady. I have come across monkeys in my day and as a race, they tend to be pessimistic, but not our gentleman. He's an optimist."

When it was time to go, I thanked Old Trad and ran all the way back to school with Garry-monkey tucked inside my coat. On the way home that evening, I was child enough to conduct an imaginary conversation on the bus. He had been very frightened, he told me, when he found I had forgotten him in Old Jethart. He knew that one day we would meet up again, but he had been lonely.

"I'm sorry, Garry," I said aloud and an elderly lady at my side turned and looked at me strangely.

"Don't take any notice of her," he advised me. "I'm so happy to see you again, to be "under your care and protection" again. Gosh! It's great. In no time, Hamish will make that money. We'll all three be together. He'll fall in love with you and you'll get married. We'll all live happily ever after."

Old Trad had told the truth about him being cheerful. If I had sad thoughts, as I sometimes had, I had only to creep upstairs to my bedroom, where I'd find him lying comfortably under the covers.

"Hello, there!" he'd call. "Isn't it a smashing day? There will be scores of cars at the ferry today. There'll be long, thirsty queues at each side. Everybody will want lemonade and crisps and chocolates . . . maybe the cars will need petrol. The tills will chink-chink-chink all day."

The next Saturday, I saved my pocket money and on Monday at lunch-time, I went to a flower shop near Old Trad's and asked what was the best thing I could buy for my cash in hand.

"Is your mummy in hospital?" she asked me and I told her that Mother was dead, told her the flowers were for a gentleman, who liked flowers, because he went to the park to look at them, when he was missing his wife and his little girl.

"The roses are the nicest, but they're expensive. You could have a fair-sized bunch of blue irises and maybe a pyrethrum or two. Have you thought of a potted plant? They last well you know."

I decided on the roses and she gave me six and added some fern for nothing. I walked into Trad's shop five minutes later and he did not hear me till I cleared my throat and then he came out and his face lit up, when he saw me.

"I never thought that I would have the pleasure of your company again, my dear lady," he said, and held the counter flap up for me to pass through. "Will you do me the honour to partake of some refreshment?"

As soon as I was in the parlour, I presented him with the flowers and made a speech which sounded far too stilted and polite. He took them from my hand and put his head down to smell them and then he looked into my face.

"Do you know this is my favourite rose?" he asked me. "It's called by the very charming name of Prosperity. So it seems that you've brought me prosperity today, and who knows that I might not take it into my head to bring it to you tomorrow? You are a very unusual and mannerly young maiden to bring me such riches, for please believe me, I have never had a present, which so moved my emotions . . . or at least I have not, for a very long time. I presume you have spent your whole week's emoluments upon my unworthy self?"

He looked at me with his bushy white brows raised and fingered his beard with his left hand.

"It's all right," I assured him. "You are very welcome. I've got Garry-monkey back and I can't believe how cheerful he is. I think you were right about adversity. Hamish has had a great deal of it and he's a super person."

"I will set about making us both a repast," he said, as he put the roses in water in an old brass vase, which suited them very well. He set them in the centre of the table and then asked me if I liked scrambled eggs on toast and if I could fancy a cup of chocolate to go with them and soon we were sitting at the table having lunch together.

"Tell me about Hamish," he said.

I never met anybody I could talk to like Old Trad, except Cousin David and of course, Hamish. You could tell him anything and he never thought you were silly or babyish. Over the next three years, I should think I told him every single thing that ever happened to me in the whole of my life. He must have come to know the Oaklands Home as well as if he had been an inmate. I told him about Mrs. Greastly and he said little children were to be pitied for their defencelessness. I can see him now standing under the low dim ceiling of the parlour, his hands outflung in one of his dramatic gestures.

"Almight God in Thy great mercy!" he cried. "Look down and weep for these your children."

I went to his shop almost every day after that and I shared his lunch and he shared my sandwiches. He showed me the things in the shop and I helped him to polish the silver and the brass. I tidied the parlour and I thought that I got it a lot better, but I could not vouch for it. I brought some of the things from the shop in to decorate the inner room and Old Trad was kind enough to tell me that I was a home-maker. We talked a lot about Hamish and I painted him in perfect colours till Old Trad laughed and took to calling him Sir Galahad. "If you ever marry him," he said to me one day, "Never take his love for granted. Tell him you love him at least once a day and if you don't want to tell him, just show him by an act of special kindness and warmth. Never let the sun go down on your wrath. Never be mean . . . never be spiteful . . . never be cruel to your fellow man." I got a kaleidoscope of wisdom from him and I never found it anything but excellent in the later years. He was my guide, my mentor and my friend and he was the one, who was to overthrow the dragon, Greastly, in the finish. It was like the mills of God grinding small, he said afterwards.

It was Jimmy McDonald, who started it. He was seven at the time the awful thing happened and he was the youngest in Auntie Jill's care. She was very kind to him, but all the same, I do not think she liked him much. Nobody liked him much. Auntie Jill told me that he was classed as "retarded" and he went to a special school because of this. He was a tiresome child, but he couldn't help it. I spent a lot of time discussing him with Old Trad, because I had to deal with Jimmy a lot and I felt disgusted very often with what I had to do for him. Old Trad lectured me about it. "God had laid the hand of his affliction on this child," he declared. "It is only by God's grace, that His hand did not rest on you."

He looked at me keenly.

"Do you understand? 'There but for the grace of God, go I.'"

I told him that I knew all that, but it didn't seem to help much. Jimmy was always soiling himself and wetting himself and it made my stomach sick to have to wash him and change his things.

"When you minister to him, you minister to Christ, my dear lady. There's a restraining thought for you. If Jimmy's nose is smeared, and you feel sick at the sight of it, recall the fact also, that it is an accident of birth that you are permitted to wipe your brother's lip and that it is not his fortune to minister to your misfortune."

He stood up and stretched his arms out by his sides.

"Mrs. Greastly will say that nobody is interested in this child," he cried. "He is mentally retarded. He drools. He is an abomination and he stinketh. Nobody in all the world cares for him. I tell you we must all care for him. He is our brother. When the bell tolls for him, it tolls for us. He is Christ come down to earth again, crucified upon his own idiocy and stoned by his fellows, who forget he has an eternal soul."

I thought about Jimmy being Christ after that, if he was particularly tiresome, and I found it was easy to get to love him. He followed me about like a puppy dog, used to creep out to the gate to wait till I arrived on the bus from school. His face came alive, when I ran down the road to put my arms round him and pick him up. I began to be glad that there was somebody waiting for me in the evenings to welcome me in.

Mrs. Greastly took it out on Jimmy because she knew I liked him. It sounds silly, written down like that, but I think it is true. She punished her victims by sharp digs in the back or playful painful pushings. If she was scolding Jimmy and I was in the room, she would look across at me and then go on hurting him, with a kind of pleasure in what she was doing to both of us. It was on my sixteenth birthday, that my hatred of her festered and broke, like an abscess, which spews out its evil over everything. I had been at the home for one year and eight months and had sat for my G.C.E. although the results were not yet in. The next term was due to start on the morrow and I was longing for it to begin. I had not seen Old Trad for six weeks and I missed him sorely. The days had consisted of long hours on the lawn with the smaller children, trying to see that they did not get into mischief.

On my birthday, Auntie Jill had seen to it that I had a cake with sixteen candles on it. I had some presents too, including a Highland bull in china from Hamish, which brought Scotland and the fields of Old Jethart right into Oaklands. There was a long letter with it and he told me that they had had a wonderful season. The weather had been hot and very tiresome for the passengers waiting for the ferry. I would soon be coming home to him. It would only take two years more and we must concentrate on all the lovely things we had to look forward to. Nobody had made any attempt to buy Old Jethart, and it was lying empty and neglected. I was not to worry about that, because it meant a reasonable price and we would soon get it round again. He had not found a suitable "porker" yet to be my adopted mother, nor was he likely to do so. Had I any opinion on the fact that dark girls were better, because he thought that might be the fact? He remained my loving Hamish and sent his love to Garry-monkey.

I went in to tea with the letter in my pocket, excited and happy, hardly able to wait for two years to pass, before I could rush back to Old Jethart. I would be eighteen, and have had a shot at the Advanced level exams. In the meantime, there was the dining room, full of happy faces, and the big white and pink iced cake, with "Happy Birthday, Belinda" written on it, and Auntie Jill at the top of our table, trying to stop Jimmy from poking his fingers into the icing on the side of it. Mrs. Greastly had been in a bad humour all the day. We had all been well aware of it and had walked with care. Poor Jimmy had been in the corner for an hour since lunch, because he spilled his glass of milk across the cloth. She frowned down the room at him from her place at the top table and told him not to spill his tea, or he would get worse.

I suppose it was all over in five minutes . . . the dreadful black thing, that was to bring her down in ruins, but it seemed to take a whole slow lifetime. Every child in the room was in high spirits. Auntie Jill was laughing at the top of her voice and we were all far too excited at our table, which ran down by the window at one side of the room. We were the envy of the others, because we had the cake, with its candles all waiting to be lit, and because it was my birthday and I was "the Birthday Queen," it was the rule, that I could do as I pleased and that nobody must be angry with me for the whole day. Our table was waited upon by the others and we sat like honoured guests and had our cups of tea brought round. We ate the bread and butter and jam and then came the Queen cakes, that Auntie Jill and I had made as a surprise. Finally I stood up and asked Jimmy McDonald to hand me the matches. He had been appointed as "Holder of the Matches for the Queen" and had been very pleased with his importance.

I struck one and lit the candles one by one. There was no sound in the room, as everybody held his or her breath with the tension of the moment. When they were all lit, there was a sigh, like wind blowing over a field of ripe wheat, I stood there and thought that there would be only two more candles on the cake on the day, that I was free to go north again. When nineteen candles were flickering on my birthday cake, I might be standing in the dining room at Old Jethart with Hamish looking along the table at me.

"Stop your dreaming, Belinda McLean!" said Mrs. Greastly sharply. "Blow the candles out and have your wish."

She was smiling with her mouth, but her voice was hard and impatient.

"Get finished and cleared away."

I do not think that a wish can ever have been granted as quickly as mine was that day. I came back to the present and looked up the room at her narrow cat's eyes. I had intended to wish to be back at Old Jethart, but before I could stop myself I wished Mrs. Greastly would be gone and that we would have a Matron as kind as Auntie Jill, instead of her.

I blew out all the candles in one blow and that sealed her fate, and Jimmy McDonald nearly went off his mind with excitement.

"You done it, B'lindy," he shrieked. "You done it. You gotcha wish. What d'ya wish for, B'lindy. What d'ya wish for?"

He sent the tea cup flying across the white cloth with a touch of his bony chapped elbow and I shall never forget the long brown stain of the tea as long as I live. Even now, I can feel hollowness in my stomach at the thought of it. It was shaped like the map of Italy and it went down the length of the cloth.

Nobody could believe that one cup of tea could do it.

For a moment, there was complete silence and then Auntie Jill jumped up from her seat.

"Oh, Jimmy!" she cried. "That's bad luck. Such a thing for you to have done on Lindy's birthday! You're far too excited, you know, but it can't be helped. It's no good crying over spilt tea, any more than it is over spilt milk. We can't put it back in the cup again, so we'll just have to pour you out another, but I do think it might be a good idea for you to marry a washerwoman, with the amount of mess you make on the cloth. Still there's no good worrying about it. We mustn't spoil Lindy's birthday over a cup of tea, even if it is all over the cloth."

We all laughed and passed it off and then I noticed that Mrs. Greastly had got to her feet and was coming down the room like a cat after a bird in a hedge.

"I told you to be careful, Jimmy," she said, swinging the accounts book in her hand, like a tawse, flicking it up and down with a snap, with the sunlight reflecting on the small metal rings in the back of it. She stood behind Jimmy and he started to cry, but it did not save him. She brought the book down across the side of his head, and he jumped to his feet and tried to run, but she grasped him by the shoulder and he started to scream in a thin shrill high way that made me lose all my sense of playing for safety.

I jumped up.

"Please don't beat Jimmy today, Mrs. Greastly," I cried. "Don't spoil my birthday."

She released his shoulder and I saw with despair that he had wet himself again and was standing with a puddle about his boots, the grey of his flannel knickers all dark down the front.

"Were you addressing me, Miss McLean?" she demanded, with her eyes bulging slightly and her face hot-furious.

I lost all sanity.

"You know he didn't do it on purpose," I screamed across the table. "He was just excited about the candles on the cake. You're mean and spiteful to take it out on him today. You've spoilt the whole party. We were all happy and now there's not a person in the room who's not miserable and near to tears. You're the cause of it all and you're glad . . . glad . . . do you hear me . . . glad!"

She came round the table in a rush like a spider and swung the book at my head, but I put up my arm and felt the metal rings tear my skin. I nursed my hurt with my other hand and saw it was bloody, although I felt no pain.

"You will please go this instant and sit at the punishment table by yourself," she said between her clenched teeth. "This is anti-social behaviour . . . birthday or no birthday . . . and it will be treated as such. You can return to your proper place tomorrow, when you have apologised to me, but you'll stay there sitting by yourself today, till you come to your senses."

I had already come to my senses. I picked up my cup of tea and walked miserably down the room, trying not to allow my shame to burn my face, full of wild rage in my heart at her unfairness and cruelty. She stalked back to her place in a deadly silence and sat down on her chair, looking smug and wrong-done-by. For a full minute, nothing at all happened. Then Auntie Jill's chair rasped back along the floor and toppled over, as she jumped to her feet.

"You mean-minded, stinking bully!" she said looking straight up the room at Mrs. Greastly. "I'll not let you do it . . . not this time. I've had enough. Come on, children, let's join Lindy. Let's all be anti-social."

She picked up the cake and marched down the room to sit at the head of the punishment table and all the children sidled off their chairs and followed her in a hesitant manner, looking back at Mrs. Greastly over their shoulders. They slid into their chairs all about me and Jimmy McDonald gave a wail of terror and flung himself into my arms. I got the smell of hot urine and thought of Christ and loved him the better. Then the children began to leave the other tables in dreadful misery and terror, creeping to join the rebellion like small sick rats. Even the children from her own table left her, sliding sideways off their chairs, their eyes never leaving her face, ready to dodge any blow she might attempt. They came down the room slowly and grouped themselves around Auntie Jill, their faces like chalk and their limbs trembling.

Auntie Jill looked all around and smiled as if nothing had happened, but I knew that she was frightened too. She knew that she had lost her job by her action and I wished she had not done it on my account.

"Lindy will now cut the cake," she said cheerfully. "Then we shall all have a slice and let battle commence."

It commenced all right, but not in the way she meant it, for Mrs. Greastly strode down the room, out of her mind with rage. Jimmy saw her coming and went into hysterics. He tore himself out of my arms and ran round the table to face her and bar her progress. He was screaming at the top of his voice.

"Go away. Go away, you dirty old cow. You're not to hit Lindy. Can't you see we all hate you. You're only a dirty rotten old cow!"

She lifted the accounts book and crashed it down on his ear and his two hands came up to try to defend his head. She lost all control of herself. She flailed him with it, and the blood came out in little points on his arms and face, where the steel rings cut his flesh. I ran round the table and fell on my knees beside him, putting my arms about him to shield him, for I thought she intended to kill him. I felt the rings flick my forehead and my bare arms and I cowered down beneath her, completely at her mercy. Auntie Jill stood up, her eyes burning blue flames in her white face. I looked up to see her stand by Mrs. Greastly and I saw the pink nylon coat tighten across her breasts as she raised the cake in the air, heavy glass stand and all. Then she cracked it down on the other woman's greasy greyish hair and I saw it splinter and break into pieces all over her head and shoulders. Mrs. Greastly went on her knees beside me and the pieces of sponge cake and icing cascaded down her full corseted bust and body to carpet the ground all around us. The heavy glass stand was a million sharp bright fragments and the blood winked out in a dozen places on her head and arms. It took a thousand years for her to collapse. She was like a monument going to pieces in front of our eyes. The great, powerful, almighty juggernaut keeled slowly over and lay on her back on the floor, snoring, her hair all about her chalk face and her skirt too high above her fat knees.

"I've killed her," said Auntie Jill in a dazed voice. "Christ Almighty! I've killed her!"

Jimmy McDonald disentangled himself from my tight embrace and went over to look down at Mrs. Greastly.

"She's still breathing," he piped in a treble voice. "You ain't done her in, Auntie Jill. Honest you ain't. She's O.K. Hark at her snorin'."

The other house mothers were crowding round with their feet scrunching on the broken glass. The cook's face appeared at the glass window in the door, that led to the kitchen. Then she came running in with her hands and arms covered with flour.

"Cor!" she said. "What's happened to Old Beastly? Who done it?"

Auntie Jill pulled herself together and grabbed my by the shoulder. She caught Jimmy's hand and pulled us both out into the corridor.

"We're all in the cart unless you do what I tell you," she said and her face was like lard. "Go upstairs, Lindy, and get the worst of the blood off yourself and Jimmy. Put on your coats and sneak out by the back way. Go down the road a bit. Don't stand outside here. Get the next bus and go in to that old fellow you're always talking about. What's his name? Old Trad. Tell him all that's happened. Don't exaggerate it one bit, even if it sounds better. Ask him what we're to do and act on what he says. For God's sake, don't let anybody catch you. It's our only chance of a fair hearing."

Jimmy and I went up the staircase, like two frightened rabbits, and I took him along to a bathroom. I got the worst of the blood off and then I put on his navy gaberdine coat and his school cap and his wool gloves.

"We haven't time to change you, Jimmy," I muttered. "I'm sorry."

I shoved my own arms into my gaberdine coat and perched the boater on my head. I put on my outdoor shoes and broke the lace on one of them, but there was no time to fix it and it slipped uncomfortably up and down on my heel. I quite forgot the bus money, that Auntie Jill had given me, and had to go back from half way down the back stairs to the windowsill in the bathroom to fetch it. My heart was thumping with fright. Every moment, I expected to see Mrs. Greastly coming up the corridor after me. Jimmy and I crept like shadows out by the back door, through the vegetable garden. In a quarter of an hour, we were safely on the bus and I was still dabbing the oozing spots on Jimmy's face and my own, with my handkerchief.

"You been fighting the cat, you two?" asked the conductor, but we said nothing and just smiled and hung our heads. We ran all the way from the bus stop in the town to Old Trad's and I was horrified to see that the shop was closed. I banged with cut knuckles on the faded brown-red door.

"Oh, God! Let him be in!" I prayed and Jimmy looked up at me, his left eye on me and his right focused on the shop window in his squinting way.

"Ain't he in then?" he sniffled. "Wot we goin' to do, if he ain't in, Lindy?"

I thumped on the door as loudly as I could.

"Please open the door, Mr. Trad," I shouted and then it opened so suddenly that I fell into his arms and put my face down among the clinking medals on his chest and wept with relief.

I do not know what he made of us, for we must have given him a shock. He took one look at our scratched, bruised faces and pulled us into the shop, shut the door behind us, led us through into the inner room, with his arms around our shoulders. He left Jimmy on a chair and then came over to me and took me by the arms and looked into my face for a moment and then he put me in his comfortable armchair and squatted at my feet.

"Shall we lave your honourable wounds first, or would you prefer to tell me how you came by them, my dear?"

"The cuts aren't bad," I told him. "But I think Auntie Jill may have really hurt Mrs. Greastly. You may have to go and save her, before they take her to jail. She sent us here to ask you what to do."

"Auntie Jill, as you call her, will get a medal, if she has destroyed that toad," he remarked with a glint in his eye. "It is high time that somebody found the courage to stamp a heel on her."

He put a cup of tea into my hands, when I had finished the story and I was shaking so much that I could not hold it, so he put an arm about me and held the cup to my lips with a smile.

"You're the same as my Sadie," he told me. "Her nerve always broke, when the battle was won, but believe me, my lady, you've struck such a blow for liberty today, or your Auntie Jill has, that the deed will re-echo down the Town and County Council Halls of the whole land."

When he had fed us and dressed our injuries, he stood with

his back to the fireplace and thought for a long time. Then he looked down at us and smiled.

"Let us consider the appointed guardians of our unfortunate children, who find themselves in need of care and protection," he said. "The Council is made up of very worthy folk and we must bring it to their notice what happens, when they appoint a dragon to see after the lambs. We've got Alderman Bullock, who hopes to be Mayor next year and will be glad to be splashed across the headlines, as a protector of the poor. There's Alderman Mrs. Mary Nottingham, who nagged her poor husband, when he was alive, and must therefore be well versed in the ways of women in authority. There's Alderman the Honourable Felicity Towchester . . . pronounced Towster, and she will give tone and breeding. Alderman Dr. Prendergast, who is retired and who had a part in filling the churchyard to capacity, before he did so, will, I am sure, tell us that this red matter is blood and that a black eye is not normal finding in a boy of seven. Let us think further . . . one or two more. Let's find Alderman Peter Flower, who is addicted to the bottle, and who does not smell as sweet as any rose and finally we'll include Alderman Billy Turner, the self-designated people's friend and champion of the poor."

He bowed towards me.

"Will you excuse me, my dear Countess, if I use my telephone to summon these acquaintances to take a dish of tea with us and I'll take it as a personal favour, Sir James, if you do your best to keep your breeks damp till the interview is at an end."

"You don't mean that I'm to pee myself a purpose?" asked Jimmy in an astonished voice.

"Don't incommode yourself on my account, my dear fellow," Old Trad smiled. "Do what you can, for of course, no man can do more and even Alderman Dr. Prendergast should know the cardinal sign of fear in those of tender age."

Of course, he knew he was on a safe wicket. He had the evidence there before their eyes, when they arrived. It is funny to look at the small white scar on my forearm now and remember that I got it on my sixteenth birthday and what a public outcry it caused when viewed by six pairs of Aldermanic eyes. It was a foregone conclusion that we would never see Mrs. Greastly again. All that remained of her was a dark stain in her sitting room, where her head used to lean back against the wall, as she sat at her desk. There was a new glass cake stand too for birthdays, to replace the one, which Auntie Jill had dumped down on top of her head. Auntie Jill acted as temporary Matron for a few weeks and we all relaxed and got a bit out of hand, and then one day, we had news of the appointment of a new warden, who was to take charge of the home, with his wife, who was to be matron.

It was strange what one person's absence could make in that big community. We were all frightened that the Greys would be like Mrs. Greastly all over again. I met Mrs. Grey first, the day she arrived and I did not meet her in the most favourable circumstances. I came back from school and walked into the play room to hear what the Warden was like, but nobody had seen either him or his wife. I heard that they had arrived at tea time and tea had been sent into the office, where they were still talking to Miss Orson, the Children's Officer. We would meet them at supper, Auntie Jill told me, and added that Jimmy had wet his trousers again and would I please take him upstairs.

"Oh, dear!" I grumbled at him. "You really do try my patience, Jimmy. Why couldn't you have asked me to take you out? Well, come on then and we'll get you into some dry things."

I took his cold red hand in mine and went through the door into the corridor and closed it after me. I walked along, towing him towards the bottom of the staircase, and then I got a sinking feeling in the pit of my stomach, for coming towards me, I saw a small dark lady in a pink nylon overall and I knew it must be Mrs. Grey. It was a bad start, and I waited for the trouble to begin. She came to a halt, when she saw us and her eyes went to the small scar below my left eye and then down to the bandage still on my arm.

"You must be Lindy," she smiled and her eyes were loving, as Auntie Jill's were.

"I had pictured you as a little girl," she said. "But you're very grown-up, aren't you, and helping the poor gentleman, who seems to have got himself into difficulties."

"I'm sorry," I said. "It's not his fault really. He tries very hard not to do it and he's much better than he used to be. Auntie Jill says that he'll soon stop altogether."

She had squatted down beside the boy in a very friendly fashion, and Jimmy was clutching the front of his pants with his hands, screwing his face up in readiness for what he thought was coming.

"What's your name?" she asked him, but he was speechless with fright, so I told her it was Jimmy McDonald. She laughed and he looked at her with astonishment.

"Well now, Jimmy," she said. "Isn't that very bad luck on our first meeting? Don't start to cry, for it's no blame to you at all and Lindy says you're getting over it. We know that you don't do it on purpose, don't we? Nobody wants to be all wet and uncomfortable, if they can help it.

She stood up and took him in her arms all damp and smelly, as he was and then she took out her handkerchief and wiped his nose, and even I, who liked him, never liked doing that with my own handkerchief. She was very trim and neat and her eyes were kind, like Trad's eyes were.

"Perhaps Lindy will show us where the things are kept," she suggested. "I'm a new girl today, so I don't really know where anything is yet. Between the three of us, we'll find a fresh pair of pants . . . an old pair for preference, and then it won't matter much if there's another accident. I think if you know it doesn't matter very much, and that nobody will be angry, it won't happen at all after a bit. Isn't that right, Master Jimmy?"

In my last two years at Oaklands, I formed an affection for Mrs. Grey, which has increased with the years. She found me telling the children one of the Old Jethart stories one evening, when I had tucked them up in their beds. It was the one I used to comfort myself, when I was lonely and it dealt with the happy time, when the estate was all made lovely again and everybody lived happily ever after. The Prince had found a fortune and had come home to Old Jethart and the children knew it as well as I did.

"And the white gate was all dirty and broken, wasn't it, Lindy?" asked Lillie Jones.

"Indeed it was," I told her. "The stock had all escaped along the road through the mountains and even the house was in a bad way."

"The slates was off the roof and the door open and the garden all nettles that sting," put in Jimmy McDonald, who had no right to be there at all, for he slept in another room, and had crept in to be by my side.

I told them how bad it was, but I said it didn't matter. In no time at all, the Prince got it looking as it had always looked. You came down the road then to the white gate and it would dazzle your eyes with its whiteness. The Prince would wait at the gate for you and his horse was black.

"That's Sultan," Jimmy added.

"As you ride up the avenue, there are sheep with queer black faces and twisted horns. They all look at you, and their eyes are witches' eyes. The Highland cattle have come home again and the hill is green and full of cowslips and primroses. Round the last bend high on the hill, the house, it's waiting, as it's waited all these years. The knocker is so polished, that it winks in the sun and there's a smell of bees' wax, from all the polishing, to welcome you in."

I told them all how it would be and then I noticed that Mrs. Grey had come in and had been listening, her face a little sad and her eyes still loving. She helped me tuck them up and bring Jimmy back to his own room and see him safely to bed and then she put an arm round my shoulders.

"You're a lucky girl to have such a place to dream about," she said. "Would you like to come down to my sitting room and we'll make tea and do toast at the fire and you can tell me all about Old Jethart and then perhaps we'll plan how to get you back there one day?"

The small room was very quiet, as I sat on the rug before the fire and told her my story. I started with Mother and the way she used to tell me about Old Jethart and then I told her about Cousin David and how he took me to Scotland. I was back there again, as I described the wonders of the place and then I came to the dark days and how I had been taken away. I went over the plans Hamish had made for us. I told her about Hamish's idea to marry somebody and adopt me as his daughter. I even told her about the remark in his letter about the dark girls and if I thought they were better, after all, than fair ones. We talked for a very long time and she didn't turn on the light, but left us in the dim light from the fire.

When I had finished, she talked to me about it all. She told me that the dream would come true. She was quite sure of it. In the meantime, she said, it was time I was allowed to grow up and she would take me shopping one of these days and see what she could do. It was Mrs. Grey, who was completely responsible for the change in the person, that met Hamish in the reception room on Christmas Eve, when I was seventeen years old and three months and in my last year at school. I am quite sure that she must have visualised Hamish and worked out what sort of a lassie he would like and then styled me to suit him. She came to tell me that he was in the reception room and that she had talked to him and liked him very much. My heart was beating so hard that I thought it might be audible, as I ran down the corridor and opened the door. I wondered what he would make of me in my tweed skirt and high-necked green sweater and the hair piled up on the top of my head. I had even used my dark lipstick and my mouth looked fuller. My nylon legs and my fringed brogue shoes were the last word in grown-up elegance.

I opened the door and went inside. Hamish was standing with his back to the Raphael Madonna and he looked at me briefly and away again.

"I'm waiting for Belinda McLean," he said.

I smiled at him down the long room and said "Are you Hamish?"

He looked towards me quickly and then came down the room.

"My God!" he said. "You're beautiful."

I ran into his arms as I always did and put my hands up to hold his face, while I kissed his cheek. Then I wound my arms round his neck and tried to choke him as usual, and he was shy with me. He made conversation. He told me about how the business was progressing and that some famous person had used the ferry and had talked to him. All the time, he avoided my eye. I would catch him stealing a glance at me and he would look away quickly.

"Mrs. Grey has asked me to stay for Christmas."

"Oh, Hamish! You will stay, won't you?"

He looked down at me and sighed.

"I can't leave you now, Corbie," he said. "I can never leave you now. Who would think that a small black crow could grow to be a beautiful and accomplished lady?"

He told me that he loved me that night after supper and he

did it in a dark Hamish-like way, that made me want to laugh and cry at the same time. He had supper with us and then he gave Mrs. Grey a look, that made me know that she knew all about it, and he led me off by the hand into the reception room once more.

He stood with his back to the fire, hands clasped behind him, a lock of his hair on his forehead, the kilt catching the light.

"I've spoken to Mrs. Grey about you," he said.

"I hope she gave me a good character."

"Aye."

His face was white and I was afraid suddenly, got in my head that he was going to be married and had come to tell me. There was no use in waiting. I asked him outright and was angry that my voice shook.

"Have you found a wife?"

"Aye."

"I'm very pleased," I lied and knew that my hopes had come to nothing. Garry-monkey had been wrong in his optimism.

"I'm pleased too."

"Is she very beautiful?" I asked him and bent my head to study the dirk in his stocking.

"Och, she's the bonniest lassie in England," he said. "I couldn't bring myself to marry a plain woman."

"She's English then?" I asked and he told me she was English born but she had good Scots blood in her.

"So you managed to find a fair lady, Hamish?"

His words were soft and warm and loving and I could not take in half he said . . . that she was the fairest woman in the land and her hair as black as a crow's . . . his wee dove, his sweet girl . . . myself, if I'd have him . . .

"If I'd have you, Hamish!"

He took my chin in his hand and looked at me.

"My! You're a bonnie lassie. It's been a long time waiting for you to grow up."

So we walked in Paradise for a while and then he took my hand and brought me back to the Christmas party in the playroom and announced very grandly that I was "his affianced bride" and I thought that maybe my troubles were coming to an end and presently he and I would be together, but my ill luck had not run out. I got two hammer blows before my eighteenth birthday, that wiped the happiness off my face.

The first was to do with Old Trad. I had been worried about him during the year, because he was far too breathless. If he walked from the parlour to the shop, he would be short of breath by the time he got there and stand with his hands pressed down against the glass, as he had stood that first day, and wait till he was breathing slowly again. His face had a blue tinge, which he tried to persuade me was the reflection from the blue battledress blouse.

"I won these in the First World War," he told me, laying his finger on the medal ribbons, "and I wore this uniform in the Second, when I was too old to carry a gun and it throws its blue tinge in my face now and tells me I'm no good for anything."

It took me three months to make him see a doctor and then he came back and told me it was good news. I was pleased and relieved.

"Then it's nothing serious?" I said.

He smiled in his old gentle, grave way and his white beard jutted out at me, while the laugh wrinkles came, deep about his wise eyes.

"If you were waiting to go to your Hamish," he said. "And God knows, you know what it is to wait . . . if you were waiting to go to him, not for three years or four, but for twenty four, and if somebody told you that the time would not be much longer, wouldn't it be the best news in the world?"

I got the old leaden feeling in the pit of my stomach, as he went on.

"I got a ticket from the doctor yesterday," he told me with a smile. "A ticket in a reserved compartment, in a given period of time . . . a ticket to go to one I've been waiting to see for twenty four long years. My bags are packed and my passport's in my hand, I'm ready to go and eager too."

I threw myself on the rug at his feet, where he sat by the fire and put my face against his knees.

"He said that you're not going to get better," I cried. "He said you're going to die. You want to see your wife again, and Sadie too, and you've forgotten all about me. Why should I lose everyone I love the best, one by one? Mother and Cousin David and now you? You can't be glad to go away from me and leave me here all alone?"

"You have Hamish," he reminded me. "When I am gone, you're to go straight to Hamish and he and his lovely bride will rule in Old Jethart in the years to come. You'll be Mistress there till you're an old, old woman, with your many years light on your white head."

"I may never get to Old Jethart again," I protested, not far from tears. "We may never get the money to buy it back again."

He caught me by the shoulders and moved me back to look in my eyes keenly.

"When I am gone," he said again. "You will go to Old Jethart and Hamish will be with you."

I hardly listened to what he said. The words poured out of me in a torrent.

"Don't wish to go away from me. You're my very best and oldest friend. Don't wish to go back to your wife and Sadie. Sadie can't want you like I do. You don't know what you've come to mean to me. Sadie and her husband are probably very happy and settled in heaven and your wife will understand how I love you. She'd be willing to wait a little . . ."

He broke in upon me.

"Sadie had no husband," he said in a black voice. "She was a child . . . a little child . . . just turned fourteen years of age the day she died. She went to your school too and the day you walked into my shop, I thought that she had come back to me from the grave."

He stood up and looked down on me, where I crouched at his feet.

"You bear a strange likeness to her in every way," he went on. "In your gentleness of manner, in your voice, in your smile, in the proud way you hold your head. It was the Almighty, in his loving kindness, sent you walking down the street that day, just to help me over the last hard, stony path of my waiting till I see them again."

I stood up then and put my arms about his neck and we wept there quietly together and I told him that I understood everything and would let him go without complaint, and the next morning, his daily woman found him dead in his bed and the first of the blows had fallen upon me.

I was just putting on my coat to go to Old Trad's shop, to see if there was any way I could help, when Mrs. Grey came into my room. She was dressed to go with me, but she carried a letter in her hand.

"It's from Hamish," she said and I thought she looked very sad. "I've had one from him on the same post. It's just as well if I tell you now, that the news is not good. It's nothing very very bad, but it will be a disappointment to you and it's a shame it had to come right on top of this other thing."

I sat on the bed and she put her arm round me, while I read the letter.

"My darling," it said. "I don't know how to write this letter to you. It seems that ill luck follows us everywhere. We must put off our goal of getting back to Old Jethart for a few more years. You know I had hoped to sell the shops to McBaynes, who were keen to have them. Jock was to have half share. I got official confirmation, that the ferry service is to be discontinued. It has not paid, so there will be no service next year and the shops are without value, as they are miles from anywhere. I must remove the petrol pumps and leave the ground as I found it and it will take a large share of our money. It will delay us, but it will not stop us. It doesn't change my feelings for you in the slightest, my darling. I loved you even as a little girl, when you came to Old Jethart, like a wild brown field rabbit, turned out of its furrow by the reaper. I may have talked about fair and beautiful maidens, with eyes as blue as skies, but my eyes never saw farther than a green-eyed lassie, who grumbled over her Latin verbs, till I had to plank down a sally switch on the table before her. I will love you till the day I die and with God's grace, for all eternity, and I curse the ill fortune which keeps us from Old Jethart. At least, we can take you from Oaklands and you will be here beside me, so that we can be together every day. I can tell you how much I love you and know that one day you'll be mine and the old house will ours, as sure as there's a moon in the sky by night and a sun by day . . ."

We laid Old Trad beside his wife and daughter in the dirty grey city cemetery the day before my eighteenth birthday and the tombstones crowded in upon us, down the sloping land on every side of us. I looked up into the weeping clouds and knew that he was not in this place of sorrows. If ever I was sure of anything, I was sure that he had found his wife again, found Sadie again . . . and happiness. The loss was mine. I had lost so many people I loved . . . Mother, Cousin David, Auld Rob, who had died of a broken heart soon after his master and now this last good friend . . .

I was in a melancholy mood the next day for my birthday, but I went through the motions of celebration . . . admired the cake, which Auntie Jill, now assistant-matron, had made, blew out every candle at once and wished that Old Jethart might be mine as soon as maybe, mine and Hamish's . . . that the time would pass swiftly.

After supper that night, I was sent for to go to the office. I wondered what was wrong, for Auntie Jill had brought the message and had told me something was up. By her face, I knew it was another birthday secret like the cake. Perhaps Mrs. Grey had arranged for me to speak to Hamish on the phone. I was sad at leaving Oaklands. If anybody had told me that such a state of emotion could have ever come about, the first day I arrived, I would have known him as a liar. Tomorrow, I knew I must leave a part of my heart here, but for now there was another birthday surprise.

There was a strange man in the office, talking to Mr. and Mrs. Grey. He stood up as I came in and looked at me curiously.

"So this is Belinda McLean?"

His face was very serious and my heart thudded. My trunk was packed upstairs. I was scheduled for a new life starting tomorrow. I was to go to Maggie and May at Innish, where they had just taken the cottage at the gates of Old Jethart. I was to lodge with them and find work and Hamish would come in the evenings. Now there was this tall man, with a gunmetal shadow on his chin and upper lip, and eyebrows like two black toothbrushes. He filled me with unease, as he put out his hand to shake mine. Mrs. Grey put her arm round my shoulders and I thought I had been wrong about the birthday secret. It had been the pattern of my life so far, these sudden disasters and I waited for one now.

"This is Mr. Stradbrooke," Mr. Grey said. "Of Stradbrooke, Stradbrooke, Waters and Stradbrooke."

Mr. Stradbrooke's hand felt like a limp, dead, rather horny fish.

"He's brought you very good news, Belinda, the most wonderful news you could ever imagine. He's called to tell you that you're an heiress. Mr. Tradworthy has left you all his money."

"I don't know any Mr. Tradworthy," I said stupidly. "It is some sort of a birthday joke, isn't it?"

Mr. Stradbrooke gave me a dry smile, which showed a row of even china teeth and told me he was Mr. Tradworthy's solicitor.

"I believe you knew my client by the name of "Old Trad". You are the sole legatee of his estate and you inherit his whole fortune, which is considerable, even in this day and age."

"Old Trad?" I said, like any parrot. "You can't mean my Mr. Trad. He was terribly poor. He lived in a poky little shop in Wassail Street and that's a poor area. He hardly ever had a customer. He sent books away to people, professors for the most part. He never liked to charge them much, because he said the right people never had any money. He used to search for first editions and they were hard to find. He never asked much profit. I used to take them to the post sometimes. He was very poor indeed."

"He was worth one hundred and twenty thousand pounds," the solicitor said in his dry as dust way. "You will inherit it, minus death duty and of course, that will be a considerable sum, but it's a great fortune and you are now a wealthy young lady. There is only one condition you must fulfil and that should not meet any objection, for I understand you had a great affection for him and he for you. He would like you to adopt his daughter's name, so that you would be Belinda Mary Stuart Sarah Tradworthy..."

"Sarah Tradworthy," I whispered. "Yes, that's poor Sadie. It is my Mr. Trad then. I hope he's with her now, with her High School blazer and the straw boater and her black hair like a crow's feather in the sun."

"Is that all you say when you've inherited as much money

as if you'd won the Pools?" demanded Mr. Grey and I went over and grabbed his and then Mrs. Grey's hand.

"What's money compared with what you've both given me for the past two years? What's his money compared to the friendship he gave me? I can never repay any of you, if I lived for ever..."

The tears rushed down my face and I went gabbling on about how they had all given me kindness and understanding and gentleness.

Then I turned on my heel and ran through the door, and up the stairs not even stopping to say goodbye to Mr. Stradbrooke. Fortunately the bedroom was empty, for it was not yet the small children's bed-time. Garry-monkey was sitting on my bed with an impossibly cheerful face.

"Belinda Mary Stuart Sarah Tradworthy McLean?" he exclaimed. "It's lucky that old Beastly hasn't to fill that one in on one of her forms."

I nodded my head and took him to his usual seat on my lap.

"I told you it would come right in the end," he went on. "But you never listened to me. Today you're rich. Tomorrow, you'll be free. Nothing to stop you buying Old Jethart, nothing in the wide beautiful world."

I held him up and looked at him with admiration and told him he was the cleverest creature known to man. He had found Old Trad in the first place and only for him I would never have met Old Trad.

I settled him back on the bed and put the covers round him comfortably and went and looked at my face in the mirror, to see if there was any difference in a poor girl and a rich girl, but there was none.

"Why don't you fly to Scotland tomorrow?" called Garry-monkey. "You could be in Innish tomorrow evening. Hamish won't be expecting you till the next day. You could have the deeds of Old Jethart to put in his hand, when you see him...

go down to the station, when the train is due in . . . give him a surprise."

Maybe I shouldn't have listened to Garry-monkey, but he had given me good advice in the years of adversity. Maybe, I should have achieved enough sophistication at eighteen, to have given up conversing with him? That's as may be. I walked into the cottage in Innish the next evening, with Garry-monkey under one arm and a handbag stuffed with five pound notes in the other. Mr. Stradbrooke had left the money for me with the Greys and we had sent a long telegram to Maggie and May, which told them I would be arriving a day earlier and that Hamish must not be told on any account.

I have never had such a welcome as they gave me on the platform at Innish. I had flown up to the airport and taken the train on. We stood on the white palings with the two collies hysterical in their delight at seeing me again. Somehow, Maggie and May had saved them from the wreckage . . . the white cat too.

Even the sun came out at the end of a dull day and made Maggie's white hair a cap of glory. The station master said that he would drop my luggage down to the cottage later and Maggie, May and I walked along the familiar, narrow, winding country road in the September evening and I knew that I had come home at last. I did not tell them about my good fortune. Hamish must be the first to hear of that. They lived in very poor circumstances in the cottage, but I was not worried about that, as I possessed the god-like power of being able to see into the future and knew that neither of them would ever want for anything, as long as they lived. They had prepared a meal for me, which touched my heart, for they had remembered all the things I liked best, even after four years. They clucked about me like two old hens about a day-old chick, which has been lost and has returned to the nest.

Then I told them that I wanted to see the old house by myself and their faces saddened.

"You'll find a sair change there," Maggie sighed.

The cottage was four hundred yards from the white gate. I walked down the road to the place where the wall curved in, and saw that the gate was gone. The driveway stood open to the road and it was choked with a sea of nettles standing two feet high. The gate was there all the same. I poked round for a few moments and came upon it, lying in the nettles on its side. It was still intact. It wanted new hinges and a fresh coat of paint and that was all. I remembered the day that Hamish had sat on it and started to fill his pipe and how I had asked "Did you know Father?" and how he had looked at me with his eyes very dark and said "I met him once or twice."

I walked through the nettles glad of my slacks and my stout shoes. In thirty yards, the drive was clear enough. It was only by the gate, that the nettles grew so thickly, and I wondered if they were meant in some weird way to bar the way to the stranger. I went along the familiar avenue, that wound round the hill and I saw the thistles and the nettles in the fields on either side and I heard Auld Rob's voice again, though he was dead and gone these three years saying "The auld hoose will mourn her and all the land aboot it will lie fallow, because she's greetin' and alane. The doors will stand open and the daws will build their nests in the tall chimneys and nettles and thistles will flood the pastures..."

The fields were empty of horses and cattle and sheep. The whole place was deserted. There were a few rooks in the trees by the house and they set up a disturbed cawing at my approach.

"Auld corbies!" I shouted at them and my voice was flung back at me from the sightless windows of the house. "Auld corbies... auld corbies... auld corbies..." it echoed.

The white door of the house stood open. Maggie had told me about the place before I left the cottage.

"There's not a body will go next nor near it," she had whispered. "Tis fu' of restless spirits. They say that a lady sings a wee bit tune and people have heard laughter a time or two . . . a man's voice. May and I, we think it's the Master and her who should have been mistress . . . It's time you knew the whole of it . . ."

That evening, I had got the last of the secrets of Old Jethart. I was old enough to understand, being eighteen turned, they said, and a grown lassie.

It all went back a long way. Did not every story about the place go back a long way, but we were back to Cool-na-Grena, mother's father's house, the "corner in the sun." It had been a fine estate, near as fine as Old Jethart, but it had come to ruin too. My grandfather had been too fond of the dram. He had ruined the family so that they came from wealth and prosperity to poverty. The two daughters, only children, were not trained to "gae oot in the world and earn their bread". My Aunt Con had come to Scotland to housekeep at Old Jethart. Folk said she had hearts for David Sutherland, but it was just talk. Mary Stuart, my mother, had come for a holiday, but she was on the look-out for work too. She was "a penniless lass wi' a lang pedigree." She had come for two weeks and stayed till she had met my father and eloped with him. Now I heard for the first time, that before that, she had been "affianced" to wed Cousin David. I had been right. They had loved each other and my father had come between them and caught her in some romantic interlude of a Hogmanay ball, with the pipes skirling, the regiment in dress uniform, the lassies in the white frocks and clan tartan stoles. Maggie and May could not know what had happened in the ill-fated match, only that Cousin David searched for her after my father's death and found . . . only me. I might paint an imaginary sketch of the true story, for I had no doubt that she loved David Sutherland. I imagined her dismay, when she found herself tied to a man, who liked the dram too much, for she had learnt what whisky can do to fields and cattle and houses and people . . . and how they can all run away into a cut-glass goblet and disappear . . .

So maybe my Aunt Con had ridden over the cliff of her own free will to find death, but I thought it likely that she had been possessed, as I myself had been possessed by Ellen Sutherland, and had had no Hamish to leap from behind a boulder to snatch her back to life . . . That was as maybe, Mother had loved Cousin David and now, "they" said that the restless ones haunted the house and had kept it an empty place, where there would be nothing "but black ruin" till a lassie came riding on a black horse to the front door, "wi her mon by her side" . . . and I had been in exile. God knows I had been in exile . . .

I stood with my hands clenched in my pockets and looked up at the neglected façade of the house, wondered if Cousin David were really there with Mother. The hairs on the nape of my neck prickled and a shiver ran down my spine. The dogs had come on a walk with me, but they shied away from the gate to the avenue. Only when I whistled them up, had they reluctantly obeyed. Now they crouched at my heels and shivered, whined, slathered a little. I walked up the six shallow steps and on through the hall into the sitting room, but Tammy and Bess crouched at the foot of the steps and whined. It was empty and lonely in the house, but there was a feeling as if somebody had been there a moment before, as if they had just gone out and would be back directly. I stood at the gate and whispered the last lines of the poem to myself.

"I love thee with the breath, smiles, tears of all my life . . . and if God wills, I shall but love thee better after death . . ."

It came down to me whispering and echoing and I looked up into the cobwebs of the greying ceiling.

"I'm back again," I said aloud and the room answered me "Back again, back again, back again . . ."

"At the very latest the day after tomorrow, I'll come riding up the avenue with my man at my side."

A sound like a sigh ran through the whole house, but it was maybe the wind in the chimney. I went across the hall into the dining room and stood where my place had been at table, thought of the high days and the holy days, the Christmasses and birthdays, and I knew it had come back, the happiness.

I walked up the stairs and at the top I turned. Through the open door, I could see Tammy and Bess crouched on their stomachs at the foot of the steps, their muzzles pointing at the sky, the whines turned to howling. I called to them to come to heel, but they only looked up at me and shivered and took to howling again, so I went into the Master's bedroom and remembered how he had lain there in his coffin and his hair silver in the light. As I thought of him, I heard a man laugh, but I recognised it for a happy memory and no sound in the world. There are strange sounds in an old house in the evenings, when the night is coming down. I came slowly down the stairs and wondered why I had not seen him before. He was there as large as life. My eyes must have been misted, to make me walk past him in the hall. He lay on the mantlepiece, with his brave yellow jumper, dirty and faded now, the yellow wool cap still set jauntily over one eye, the brown knit trousers, that Mother had made. It was Garry-monkey, the pessimist, staring up at the ceiling, high and dim above him, from the place they must have flung him, as they moved the furniture out. I picked him up gently and looked at the blackberry boot-button eyes in the woebegone face, now powdered with dust. I shook him and a cloud of it pricked my nostrils and made me sneeze. I took out my handkerchief and polished his eyes. He was wonderfully as I remembered him. His clothes smelt musty, but that could soon be remedied. The whole house smelt musty and that could be remedied too. I sat down on the bottom step of the stair and thought of Old Trad and the way he had given me Sadie's favourite toy. It must have been one of his most precious possessions, yet that first day, he had given it to me freely . . . later her name, then his whole huge fortune, but the toy monkey would have meant the most to him. He had seen how much it meant to me and thrown his need and mine into the balance . . .

"I've got a friend, I want you to meet", I said. "He's called Garry-monkey too, but he's an optimist. I'll introduce him to you presently, but maybe his name wasn't Garry-monkey at one time. Old Trad was gracious enough to let it be . . ."

He looked up at me as blankly as ever and his voice cracked at not being used for so long.

"I'm glad to see you again," he said. "I knew you'd come back for me. I wasn't worried . . . knew you'd appear up those steps with fame and fortune. All we've got to do now, to let Auld Rob rest easy, is to find a black horse and Hamish . . . and buy the place. Oh gosh! In ten years, the house will be full of children. I'll thank you not to let them play with me, for I've had enough adversity . . ."

I heard the laughter again and knew it for a figment of the imagination, or thought I knew it. A woman's voice began to sing, a high, light, gay little voice, that sang as Mother used to sing . . .

> "I had a little nut-tree, nothing would it bear,
> But a silver nutmeg and a golden pear.
> The King of Spain's daughter came to visit me
> And all for the sake of my little nut-tree . . ."

It was a whisper, hardly a sound, the wind in the trees about the house, the calling of the gulls far out to sea, an echo of the past.

"Mary Stuart," I whispered, "Mary Stuart . . ."

I felt her all around me, warm, soft and comforting, as she had been in the old days, with her arms about me and her voice saying "Don't fret, honey . . ."

The dogs had ceased their howling and were slinking off

down the avenue, ashamed to be quitting my defence, but this was no intruder they could challenge. I tucked Garry-monkey under my arm took the front steps in one leap. I was happy, happy, happy, happy. I strode off along the avenue after the dogs, singing as I went.

> "I had a little nut-tree, nothing would it bear,
> But a silver nut-meg and a golden pear..."

It was not a good marching song. After a while, I skipped to it, danced to it and so I went along, with the dogs recovered from fear now and jumping at my side. I arrived at the cottage, dusty and breathless and held Garry-monkey out to Maggie and May.

"Look who's been steward at Old Jethart till we came back."

"It's not possible!" cried Maggie. "It's just not possible."

I went to the Estate Agent the next morning early and told him what had happened. He was a stranger, who had come new to the district and he did not know me. He said the same thing as Maggie.

"It's not possible!" he said. "It's just not possible!"

I looked at him in amazement.

"Old Jethart was sold yesterday," he told me.

"It must be possible!" I protested, "I have the money. At least, I haven't got it on me, but the solicitor will send it to you, if I write to him."

"I'm sorry, lassie, the property's sold."

"It can't be sold," I cried. "It's a haunted house. Nobody would buy it. Everybody knows it's unlucky. If somebody else has bought it, not knowing the superstition, I'll buy it back. I'll give twice what he paid for it, if necessary. Who is it? I'll go talk to him."

"I canna gie ye information aboot clients," he said sourly. "It's a private transaction. I canna broadcast to any Tam,

Dick or Harry who's bought property in the market, or I'd do sma' trade."

"I'll give him twice the price he paid for it," I argued. "I told you."

"It's na the money he's after," he said dourly. "I can tell ye that much. I think he's acting agent for a body, that's made o' money. I reckon he wants it for the feshin' and the shootin'."

He turned his back on me rudely and I leaned over the counter and grabbed his shoulder.

"If I speak to him, he'll not be hard-hearted enough to refuse me," I cried. "Cousin David and my mother are haunting that house. They're still there. I heard them there myself last night. I heard her singing the song and I heard him laughing, just as he always laughed. They'd be miserable if a stranger has the place. They'd not rest easy..."

He turned round very slowly and removed my hand from his shoulder and looked at me through his gold rimmed spectacles.

"Are ye daft, lassie?" he asked me.

I glared back at him for a few moments and then I put my hand into my bag and took out a wad of five pound notes. It was all I had with me and I was being very foolish and I knew it too. I laid the money on the counter.

"You can have that, if you give me the name of the man, that bought it," I said through my clenched teeth.

He lost his temper with me.

"Ye *must* be daft," he said, his lips curling. "To throw guid money like yon aboot. Ye canna bribe me wi' it, so ye can put it awa', in the wee sack again. I'll tell ye one thing. The man, that's bought it, is a mighty dour, canny character and he's just as detairmined as ye are, yersel', to have the farm. He'll no' change his mind, and it's no good yer wasting yer time and his and mine too, so awa' hame wi' ye noo."

I begged. I prayed. I coaxed. I almost went down on my

knees to him. Then I altered my tactics. I told him I was a rich woman. I could buy the whole village if had a mind to, I said and raised my nose an inch into the air.

"Ye'll no' buy Old Jethart," he laughed. "For 'tis no' for sale!"

I climbed up on the high counter then and settled myself down comfortably. I glared at him.

"I will not leave your office till you tell me who's bought it," I declared. "I'll sit here dangling my feet till you give in. I'll have my food sent in to me and I'll stay here day and night, if it's necessary."

"Ye'll no' do that either," he said and lifted his lip, in what he thought was a smile. It made him look more like a wolf than ever.

"I've three lassies at hame," he went on. "Twice as big as you are, and I can deal wi 'them quite handy. You'll no' be able to sit doon to yer dinner, let alane on my counter, if ye're not oot in yon yard in two seconds. I'll put ye across my knee, big and all as ye are, and I'll dust yer backside for ye fine. My lassies will tell ye I've got a hard hand for the job. They've no' to be told to dae a thing twice."

"You wouldn't dare!" I said in a rage.

"Would I no?" he said with another of his wolfish smiles. "I'll dae more for ye. There's a pump oot in the yard yonder and a nice trough o' watter below it. I'll drop ye in there, when I'm done wi' ye. 'Twill cool your pairson off a wee, before ye set oot doon the road to yer hame."

He would have done it too, for I had made him very angry. He took a step towards me, and I leaped off the counter and walked to the door.

"Keep away from me," I warned him, my voice breaking, I faced him with my hand on the door handle.

"You'll be sorry for this day's work. I'll buy the whole of Innish and if it's the last thing I do, I'll ruin you. Then you and your three big daughters and their 'sair' backside can go to hell!"

He made a run at me then, and I went through the door with no dignity at all.

"Mon! Ye'r a hoity-toity miss!" he called after me and I looked back from a hundred yards down the road and saw him standing in the doorway, his hands on his hips. I found out afterwards, that he had a queer sense of humour. He was a single gentleman, who had lodgings at the Manse and his indigestion troubled him sorely, till he married May three years later. They have a small daughter now, who turns him round her little finger and never gets corrected verbally, let alone physically, and we are the best of friends.

I went back down the road to Maggie and May in the little stone cottage and I gave them such a picture of the Land Agent, that it is a wonder May ever wed him. I still had not told them of my inheritance. They thought that I had gone to enquire about the price of the estate. I mooned about the place till well past teatime and was pretty miserable with one thing and another.

Maggie was worried because I ate only one of her hot buttered scones, so I could not very well refuse a slice of the Dundee, and it nearly choked me. As far as Hamish knew, I was due in on the evening train and he was to meet me on the platform. After tea, I decided that I would go back to Old Jethart for the last time, so I put on my slacks and sweater and the stoutest shoes I possessed and I told them I was going for a walk and would then collect Hamish at the station and bring him back to supper.

Half the gladness was gone out of my life and although I knew I was being very foolish not to be wild with joy at the thought of seeing Hamish again, I knew that I was betraying the old house if I married him and went away and never came back again to see it, except as a visitor. I had no choice, but my heart was heavy. I stood on the gravelled drive and looked up at the face of Old Jethart and tried to say I was sorry I had failed. It had a decrepit melancholy about it. The sky was overcast. Even the rooks were silent. I kicked my toe on each of the steps, as I went up to stand in front of the door. It was a thing I had done as a child to bring good luck. The knocker of the door, the handle, the letter box were all black-green with neglect. I went into the hall, on into the sitting room. I knelt down by the fireplace and remembered how often I had knelt thus to dry my hair and I wondered if Cousin David was sad, because I would come to the house in future and stand on the outside, looking in, with no right to enter it any more. I could not feel his presence about me, as he had been the evening before. I got to my feet, the old aching in my throat and went into the dining room as if I searched him out. I stood in his place and raised my hand, as if I held a glass.

"To absent friends," I said in a voice, which echoed again round the emptiness of the whole house.

"To absent friends," I repeated and thought of them . . . named them one by one, as if I summoned them to earth again.

"Mother," I said. "Poor Mary Stuart . . ."

I remembered Auld Rob out on the cliff top.

"Come awa' hame, lassie. Ye'd not know whit was listening to ye."

"Cousin David . . ."

"Whit if he were to answer ye?" Rob had asked that night.

"Auld Rob, wise, loyal, too faithful to outlive your master."

The house was empty. There was no feeling that somebody had just quit the room and must soon come back again. They had all gone, the gay spirits, and I was still intent on "absent ones."

"Old Trad, my dear, dear friend . . ."

I thought how he had made it possible for me to survive the exile. It must have been a shock to him that day, when I walked into his shop, when he came from the inner room and saw Sadie there, in navy gaberdine coat and the hat with the school ribbons . . . and he had given me the toy monkey, who liked to sit in the window to watch who came along the street.

"I'll come back here one day, and only because you've made it possible. You taught me patience . . . Do you think I'm foolish to stand here talking to an empty house? I'm sorry, but even the luke-warm furnaces of adversity haven't cured me of self- pity."

I went upstairs slowly, a step at a time and it was as if they had willed happiness to me. My mood was sunny all at once, as it had been the evening before, and even the sun broke out of the clouds.

"Hamish will fix it," I thought to myself. "He can fix everything fine. We'll be back one day and if not, Hamish nor myself . . . our children will come. I'll build a vision of it in their hearts, as Mother did in mine. They'll not rest easy till it's ours again. I'll tell them of the white gate with the special latch, of the way the avenue winds in through the trees, till it turns round the hill . . . and the square house with the white door, that stands proud, and the river and the mountains . . . the silent mountains, sentinel . . ."

I stood in the landing window that looked down on the steps, saw the river and across the fields to the far sea, saw the golden path of the sun to the horizon and the way the earth caught the gold in its drowsy hand and threw it down in molten fire between the house and eternity.

"I'm going now, for I've no choice but to go. I swear that I'll come back, I, or my kin . . . if not I, my daughter or my daughter's daughter, will come through that gate with her man by her side. Old Jethart will come back to its ain folk in the end of it all."

I heard a man laugh and there was somebody with a swinging kilt running up the steps, as Cousin David had done, when he came home.

"I had a little nut-tree, nothing would it bear,
But a silver nut-meg and a golden pear . . ."

It was Mother's voice, but it was I, who sang. I turned down the stairs and half way down, I saw him standing in the hall. He stood there, where he had always stood, the light shining in behind him, making a halo round his head and a spectrum of colours round his kilt.

I was afraid of him suddenly. Why should I fear Cousin David, because he had come back from the past to talk to me? The song died in my throat and my mouth was dry. I could not will myself to go to him. He came across the hall and stood at the foot of the stairs.

"Corbie!" he said, and I saw that Cousin David was a trick of the setting sun. Hamish it was, and my heart was racing as it always raced when I met him again.

"You scared me witless. I heard that song they say your mother sings. I thought you were a ghost."

He looked up at me.

"What the hell are you doing up there? You're supposed to be on the train in half an hour."

"I thought you were a ghost too," I murmured.

"Stop talking nonsense," he laughed. "Come down here this minute."

I jumped the last four steps into his arms and thought what a wondrous thing it was that we would soon be wed. I wondered if we would find such pleasure in each other's company till the day we died, and like all lovers, knew that we would. We went out after a while, sat ourselves down on the steps and he forgot to ask me again why I was not on the train. We were both so taken up in telling each other how happy we were going to be that I forgot to tell him my news and he forgot to tell me his. We sat there till the darkness came down and his kisses were long and warm on my mouth. I sighed at last and got to my feet, said it was long past the time when we should have reached the cottage. We stood hand-in-hand and looked up at the old house.

"We must say good-bye to Old Jethart," I said sadly. "But we'll be back if it takes us fifty years."

"What are you blethering about?" he demanded. "We'll be back tomorrow and the day after and the day after that."

I shook my head miserably and said that I had forgotten to tell him.

"It's not for sale," I said. "Somebody else bought it and he's keeping it. There no chance of getting it back, even if we gave him twice the money. We'll have to have patience. If we can't live there, our children will or our children's children. I've thought it all out. Don't fret about it, Hamish, for it's no good. We'll be wed soon, as you just said. Waiting will be easier, when we have each other. The loneliness for Old Jethart won't be so bitter for us. We'll find somewhere else and we'll wait till we can come home."

"Are you gone out of your wits?" he demanded.

I looked up at him and remembered Old Trad's will.

"Of course, you don't know about it. I got some money. Old Trad left me a fortune. It was to be a surprise, but it's all gone flat. I came by plane and I saw the agent. He's stubborn and he's disagreeable. I couldn't do anything with him and it's hopeless. He'd never understand how much we wanted it and the other chap would never sell, the chap who's bought it."

"The chap, that bought it, would never sell it," Hamish agreed but he cared not a jot, one way or the other.

"So you know about it? Do you know who he is?"

"Och! I know him well," said Hamish, turning his back on me.

He did not want me to see his face, any more than I wanted him to see mine.

"Is he young or old? Is there any chance of him dying soon?"

"I don't think we should wish for that," Hamish said, in a pious kind of way.

"If you tell me who he is, I'd go and see him . . . tell him the whole story. Would it be any good?"

"He's a dark chap, stubborn as a mule," Hamish said. "You might get round him to do almost anything, but he'd not sell Old Jethart. He's been after it for years."

His shoulders were shaking and I thought it awful that he should weep. He cared for it, just as I did. He knew there was no happiness away from Old Jethart, even if we were together. I put my arms around him and leaned my face against the rough tweed of his jacket.

"Don't fret, Hamish. I have a great deal of money. We'll give it all to this man and we'll get Old Jethart back. Don't weep for it, my darling."

He spun round and grabbed me into his arms, spoke fiercely into the top of my head.

"If you were to marry him and he'd have you too, for he's had his eye on you since you were small, if you were to marry him, you'd be mistress of Old Jethart and not a penny spent of your 'Great deal of money'."

"I'll wed nobody but you," I muttered against his neck. "If we can't have it, our kin will, our children, our grandchildren."

"Are you talking of grandchildren and we not wed yet?" he demanded in a shocked voice, but he sounded mighty cheerful for a man, who had been weeping.

He set me aside and took the six shallow steps in one bound. Then he turned round to face me with a swirl of the kilt. In the gloaming, the house behind him was regenerated to its old grandeur.

"The ferry's not to go. We sold it to McBaynes' for a fortune . . . enough and to spare. I bought the place yesterday. We'll see they live happily ever after, Maggie and May, Jock McGregor, Jimmy McDonald, the two collies and Lady Judy, and the white cat, and yourself and myself, you and your two Garry-monkeys. God above! Wouldn't you think you'd have more sense and you a woman grown, but not one Garry-monkey now but two, and talking to them still. Och, lassie! I love you!"

He stretched his arms to the sky and then set his fists on his hips. He was the king of the whole world as he looked down the steps at me and grinned.

"Have ye no' a mind to come up here and kiss the black Master of Old Jethart?" he said.